LANDFALL 248

November 2024

Editor Lynley Edmeades

Reviews Editor David Eggleton
Founding Editor Charles Brasch (1909–1973)

Cover: Simon Richardson, *Vincent O'Sullivan*, 2022.

Published with the assistance of Creative New Zealand.

OTAGO UNIVERSITY PRESS

CONTENTS

- 4   Landfall Essay Competition 2024 Judge's Report, *Lynley Edmeades*
- 6   Unsteady Ground, *Franchesca Walker*
- 16   Response to a Restructure, *Hannah August*
- 27   aye i, *Elese Dowden*
- 28   Long Distance, *Perena Quinlivan*
- 29   Kukutauaki, *Janet Newman*
- 30   Pendulum, *Keith Nunes*
- 31   Dog Days, *Isabel Haarhaus*
- 38   Viewpoint, *Eliana Gray*
- 39   Mother, *Tess Ritchie*
- 40   Window, *Cilla McQueen*
- 41   Habits (La Bohème), *Cadence Chung*
- 42   Asks, *Atareria*
- 43   The Sound of the Universe, *Rebecca Reader*
- 49   Oxygen, *Megan Kitching*
- 50   Thirteen Beautiful Things, *Josiah Morgan*
- 51   Lesbians at a Mormon Dance Party, *Kim Cope Tait*
- 54   King Kamehameha, *Kirby Wright*
- 55   In the Company of Bullies, *Breton Dukes*
- 62   Coming to the End of the Red Apple, *Jessica Le Bas*
- 63   Sisyphus at Kā Roimata o Hine Hukatere Glacier, *Joanna Pascoe*
- 65   That Stage, *Brent Kininmont*
- 66   Company Rule, *Jackson C. Payne*
- 74   The Lantern of Fear Sausage Sizzle, *Rachel O'Neill*
- 75   The Fat Girl, *Shelley Burne-Field*
- 83   DARVO, *Erik Kennedy*
- 84   study, *Mary Macpherson*
- 85   from Animal Etymologies, *Vana Manasiadis*
- 86   Poplar, *Mark Edgecombe*
- 87   The White Colt, *Diana Bridge*
- 88   ART PORTFOLIO, *Simon Richardson*
- 97   Vincent, *Michael D. Jackson*
- 102 flood, *Cindy Botha*
- 103 The Halo Effect, *Hannah Petuha*

111 No Solutions for your Illness, *Holly Fletcher*
112 ART PORTFOLIO, *Heidi Brickell*
121 The Arisen, *David Eggleton*
122 7 October 2023, *Philip Temple*
123 Clearance, *Tony Beyer*
124 Awakening, *Medb Charleton*
125 Separation, *Frankie McMillan*
126 The Years, *Anna Woods*
133 oubliette, *Sherryl Clark*
134 Best in a Sheltered Spot, *Brett Reid*
135 Caselberg Trust International Poetry Prize 2024 Judge's Report, *Alan Roddick*
137 The Valley Where Compassion Died, *Rangi Faith*
138 Time of Death, *Philip Armstrong*

139 MAKING SPACE: IN COLLABORATION WITH RMIT UNIVERSITY'S non/fictionLab
140 Two Improvisers Walk into a Bar, *Es Foong and Ambika G.K.R.*
149 Intergenerational Spaces and Trans-Tasman Places, *Sholto Buck and Stayci Taylor*
162 Vertical Dialogue, *John Kinsella and Robert Sullivan*

THE LANDFALL REVIEW
174 Landfall Review Online: Books recently reviewed
175 ROBERT SULLIVAN on *Katūīvei: Contemporary Pasifika poetry from Aotearoa New Zealand* edited by David Eggleton, Vaughan Rapatahana and Mere Taito
177 EMMA GATTEY on *Gauguin and Polynesia* by Nicholas Thomas
182 DAVID HERKT on *Marlow's Dream: Joseph Conrad in Antipodean ports* by Martin Edmond
186 MICHAEL HULSE on *Still Is* by Vincent O'Sullivan
190 ELIZABETH SMITHER on *Bird Child & Other Stories* by Patricia Grace
193 DAVID EGGLETON on *An Indigenous Ocean: Pacific essays* by Damon Salesa

203 CONTRIBUTORS
208 LANDFALL BACKPAGE, *Christopher Schmelz*

LYNLEY EDMEADES

Landfall Essay Competition 2024 Judge's Report

This is the third year I've had the privilege of judging the annual Landfall Essay Competition, a job that certainly does not get easier with time. There were a record 126 entries this year and at least 30 potential winners. A different month, a different season, a different judge, and I'm sure the results of this competition would have shaken out in quite a different way. I've never been good at drawing a line in the sand; I drew a wobbly one this year and chose two essays as joint winners.

Franchesca Walker's essay 'Unsteady Ground' floated very quickly to the top of my 'definitely a placegetter' pile and continued to reward with every subsequent reading. On one level, it deftly explores the challenges of putting back together the jigsaw of a fractured whakapapa, particularly from beyond the shores of one's own whenua. On a deeper level, Walker's essay shows what happens when a culture is silenced, when emotional and psychic lives are repressed. Walker weaves together pieces of her great-grandfather through fragments of memory, apocryphal stories and journalistic interpretations, constructing a valuable mosaic of a man who was made subject to the many overbearing powers of his time. With the lightest of touches, she then prompts the reader to think about how the fragments of our ancestors live on within us and how the fractures and fissures then may be playing out in our waking life. Her great-grandfather comes to her in dreams, as forcefield, as protector. But the things that he and her predecessors endured never go away: as Walker says, 'Their lives were the nutrients that fed me as I grew. The things they left unsaid shook the earth beneath my feet.'

Hannah August's 'Response to a Restructure' is a beautiful polemic—in superbly written prose, the author meditates on love and the humanities, drawing our attention to the act of silencing by institutional power in the interest of profiteering models. It also makes a superb argument for the place of the public intellectual, which we need now more than ever before. I've read previous essays by August and continue to appreciate that she never shies away from her own intellectual prowess. Her writing is gentle and affective, authentic and unashamedly subjective, likely the closest I've read in Aotearoa to an autotheoretical essayistic mode of writing—reading the world through the self, where that self contains multitudes of emotional and theoretical layers. As someone fortunate enough to have a job in academia, I am so grateful for the kind of serious thinking that August is doing around the dire state of our national governmental tertiary policies and the ramifications for humanities departments across the motu. This essay is as soothing as it is empowering.

I chose these two essays not only because I couldn't decide between the two pieces—the more I tried to hold them up against each other, the more they fought their corner—but also because I believe they speak to the same set of issues. When I put them side by side, I started to see some threads of connective tissue, furthering the necessity of multiplicities and polyphony. In their different ways, both essays suggest that manipulating ideologies for the purposes of expansion and control—either colonial or capitalist—will always have an effect. If Freud has taught us anything it is that repression, of the individual or the collective, will only ever result in disaster; those feelings, attitudes, or ideas will always find a way out again, and will return in uglier and more odious ways. The more we can attune to the voices of our past—both collective and individual—the more fight we might have in us to endure the weight of the present and to effect positive change in the future.

First place
Franchesca Walker, 'Unsteady Ground'; **Hannah August**, 'Response to a Restructure'

Third place
Kate Duignan, 'Submission'

Highly commended
Joan Fleming, 'Seven Lots of Bad'; **Amelia Reynolds**, 'Method Acting'; **Catherine Russ**, 'Dog Days'; **Diane Brown**, 'Phantom Rain and Other Uncomfortable Ghosts'

Commended
Julie Hill, 'Splashed by Spray'; **Rebekah Galbraith**, 'Good Luck, Babe!'; **Majella Cullinane**, 'Cured'; **Marilyn Wright**, 'Skin'

FRANCHESCA WALKER

Unsteady Ground

> WALKER, Barry. Sadly passed away on Sunday, August 6, 2017 at home, surrounded by family. Aged 83 years. Mate of Sandy (deceased). Loved father and father-in-law of Martin, Anita (deceased), Trevor and Jillian, Apikara and John, Junior and Aroha, Oriana and Stephen. Beloved Gampsy of all his mokopuna. Barry will lay at Aotea Marae, Makirikiri, Dannevirke. A service will be held at The Church of Jesus Christ of Latter Day Saints, Cole Street, Dannevirke on Thursday, August 10, 2017 at 11am followed by a burial at Tahoraiti Urupa.[1]

The pine trees lining the driveway bowed in the wind as the hearse drove onto the urupā. My cousins unloaded Gamps's casket and carried him through the entrance, skirting the ground pock-marked by old burials. Dad's eyes watered as we followed them in, but when my partner Alex handed him a tissue and nodded at the tears on his cheeks, he immediately blamed the wind.

    They climbed into the neighbouring paddock to lower Gamps into his grave. Wedged between his parents' headstone and the edge of the urupā, there wasn't anywhere else they could stand. The top wire sagged as my cousins leant over the fence and let the ropes slip through their hands. I watched the edge of the grave nervously, wondering if the wet winter soil would give way beneath them—after years living in Western Australia, I could no longer judge the stability of the ground. Behind them, cloud shadows sped across unbroken farmland while, in the distance, Ruahine Range hunched into the earth.

I was never close to my grandfather. If I'm being honest, I never really knew him, kept at arm's length by his gruffness, complicated relationship with my father, and one-eyed determination to muscle through the boot camp he called life.

    In his prime, he was broad-shouldered. Arms and legs like tree trunks. The saying 'built like a brick shithouse' comes to mind. My uncles and aunties used to tell how, aged just 13, his father James Te Teira took him scrub cutting in the Wairarapa back blocks and left him there to fend for himself. Alone for weeks, he guarded the camp and hunted for food. According to one version, he shot and skinned dozens of deer, hoping to claim the government's skin bonus once he got back to town. The story was told as evidence of Gamps's innate strength and durability. Barely a teenager and already able to look after himself in the bush. *He stayed out there for weeks*, my uncle said in a voice suggesting he'd never do the same. *Tough, aye? Had to be damn tough.*

We called him Gamps because, as a toddler, my eldest cousin had struggled to say 'Grandfather' or even the more casual 'Gramps'. To be fair, neither of these titles would have fit him. Grandfather conjured images of a stately, house coat-wearing elder who spent his days reading; Gramps, a kindly person who kept lollies in his cardigan pocket to share with his grandchildren when they came to visit.

Gamps swore constantly and with great gusto, using four-letter expletives where others would have opted for words like 'very' or 'really' or 'just'. Everyone was a bastard—his friends, his family, the horses he bet on each week that failed to cross the line in a timely manner. He'd drag out the first half of the word, wrapping his mouth around the long vowel, then slap you across the face with the final syllable.

Yet Gamps barely spoke when we visited him and Nan. He'd generally ask me and my siblings one question when we first arrived—how was school going, maybe, or whether we'd won our most recent game of netball or soccer—then, duty done, he would only acknowledge us when ordering us to the table for kai or to bring him a beer from the fridge. I used to watch him, peering into the lean-to where he and the rest of the family drank, wondering what happened to all the words he left unsaid. Sometimes, it felt like they were silently filling the house and pushing out all the oxygen. I'd find myself gasping for air and wondering where it all went wrong.

After my cousins finished back-filling Gamps's grave, I walked over and stood awkwardly next to him, unsure what to say or do. He didn't have a headstone yet—that would come in about a year—so I couldn't even pretend to read the inscription. Some soil had spilled onto the grave next to him, so I nudged it with my foot, pushing it back to where it belonged. As I did, I caught sight of the neighbouring grave's headstone:

EMERE PIRIHA WALKER JAMES TEIRA WALKER
DIED 17ᵀᴴ APRIL 1943 DIED 8ᵀᴴ FEB. 1952
AGED 32 YRS. AGED 56 YRS.

NA TE WA KA KITE ANO

Emere and James Te Teira: Gamps's parents; my great-grandparents.

I bent down and traced James Te Teira's name with my finger. For years, my great-grandfather's photo hung on Nan and Gamps's living room wall. He stood behind a tennis net with three other men. Two of them held rackets while James Te Teira had a pad and pencil, presumably for keeping score. He wore white shoes, white pants, a white handkerchief tied around his neck, and a black blazer with white piping on the cuffs and lapels. He smiled. The sun bounced off his forehead, casting shadows over his eyes.

When we stayed the night at Nan and Gamps's, I would scrunch down in my sleeping bag on the living room floor, breathing in the carpet's dry, sandy smell. Music filtered through the windows—often Engelbert Humperdinck's *Please Release Me* with backing vocals from my uncle and great-aunty, who would've got into the Scrumpy earlier that evening. There was no point trying to sleep, so instead I spent my time staring at James Te Teira's photo. Looking at him was like seeing Dad's face—Gamps's as well—from the bottom of a river. He had the same prominent forehead, the same eyes that creased when he smiled, the same oval-shaped face.

I would count the things I knew for certain about him. They fit on one hand.

Thumb: he came from Nūhaka, a small east coast settlement in the heart of Ngāti Rakaipaaka territory.

Index finger: he spent a good chunk of his life living at Mākirikiri, on the outskirts of Dannevirke.

Middle finger: when he died, he chose to be buried at Tahoraiti urupā, even though his mother, father, brothers and sister lay back in Nūhaka.

My ring finger and pinkie didn't hold any facts about James Te Teira.

Back in Australia after Gamps's tangi, I dream about my family. They move from room to room, reciting karakia as they cleanse a house, freeing spirits who have become stuck within its walls. Although I can't make out their exact words, their prayers are comforting, and I find myself drifting, carried on the sound of their voices and the safety of their presence.

Suddenly, the dream changes. My family disappear and, scanning the room, I find I'm completely alone. My heart starts racing and it's like some sort of signal because a kēhua appears. The ghost reaches out its hand and tries to touch me with a single extended finger. I recoil and scramble away, but my back smacks against a wall and there's nowhere else to go. It moves closer, reaching for my face. Instinctively, I shut my eyes tightly and begin screaming Gamps's name over and over and over again. Not because I think he is the kēhua but because somehow I know, deep down, he's the only one who can save me.

Walker Gets Damages

Further Evidence In Assault Case

JUDGE POINTS TO JURY'S RESPONSIBILITY

> General damages of £30, with special damages amounting to £33 12s 6d (medical, and dental expenses and loss of wages) were awarded to James Walker, of Makirikiri, the Hawke's Bay ex-rep. footballer, who was plaintiff in the assault case which came before the Hon. Mr. Justice Reed and jury at the Palmerston North Supreme Court on Thursday and yesterday. Walker, who is a three-quarter-caste Maori, alleged that eight Maoris of Makirikiri pah, near Dannevirke, had conspired to assault and beat him and on July 15 of last year between 5 p.m. and 6 p.m. had actually set upon him with fists and fencing battens with the result that he regarded it was only by the greatest fortune that he had not been killed.[2]

After I dreamt about Gamps and the kēhua, I started tracking James Te Teira through the internet. I typed his name into genealogy websites and archival search engines. I spent Perth's long winter evenings picking up traces of him in war records, articles about rugby, references to court proceedings.

It wasn't easy because he'd been known by so many names. In primary school, he was recorded as Teira Walker. When he enlisted in the First World War, he signed his name 'Jimmie'. And when his first wife petitioned him for a divorce, the Māori translation of the court documents called him Hēmi Te Teira Walker. Every mention felt like a breadcrumb, a clue he'd left behind especially for me. I carefully filed the documents I found on my computer in folders labelled 'Nūhaka', 'Rugby', 'Assault' and 'Divorce'. Every month I added more to each.

I couldn't say how my research was related to the dream—or if it was related at all—but once I started searching for James Te Teira, I didn't dream about kēhua again.

> The defendants … denied the conspiracy but stated that on July 8 (a week before the assault) a meeting of Maoris of the pah had been held to inquire into the conduct of Walker with one Emere Karaitiana, wife of Tame Karaitiana. Walker was requested to leave the woman alone. However, he refused to give any promise and had said nobody would stop him having any woman he wanted whether married or single … Defendants were members of the Young Maori Association at Makirikiri and as a result of the plaintiff's conduct the association decided to request him to leave the pah. Walker refused, and abused and attacked defendants.[3]

Growing up, there were stories I heard about James Te Teira. Apocryphal stories, used to explain the hows and whys of our family, ones that lived in the throwaway lines of my father, uncles and aunties.

We apparently didn't grow up speaking te reo Māori because James Te Teira was shamed for speaking it when he first moved to Dannevirke and was so upset he pledged to never teach his children Māori ways. None of the men in our family played rugby beyond high school, apparently, because James Te Teira once told Gamps you had to give it up when you got married. James Te Teira had played representative rugby for Hawke's Bay and travelled overseas with the Māori All Blacks, but they said it broke up his first marriage, took him away too often, occupied his mind.

This first marriage was used to explain Gamps's seemingly never-ending stream of brothers and sisters. It was said both his father and mother had been married at least once before they first met, although exactly how they met or, more importantly, when they met was shrouded in mystery. Gamps once explained his beginnings this way: *My father came sneaking around here, and then there was me.* Recently returned from a stint in hospital, Gamps was lying in the room where he had been born, in the house his mother, Emere, had built at Mākirikiri before James Te Teira stormed into her life.

Medical Evidence

Dr Maclaurin gave evidence concerning the injuries plaintiff had suffered, including large contusions on the head. There was a lump an inch high and 2½ inches long on the forehead, besides extensive abrasions and contusions on the arms and chest and some dental damage. The head wounds were consistent with his being struck with a piece of wood, and those on the body with kicks. He had been roughly handled, but was exceptionally strong. He showed signs of a serious assault.[4]

A digitised newspaper article taught me about the time James Te Teira was beaten by his neighbours. My family never mentioned it, even though the spot where it took place was only 100 metres from Gamps's childhood home—the home in which Emere had lived when James Te Teira began 'sneaking around'. My family never mentioned it, even though my uncle had lived in Gamps's childhood home as I was growing up, and we drove past the spot every time we visited him.

Dad, it turned out, had always known about the beating, although he was a little unclear about why it had happened. I met up with him and Mum for dinner at a tapas restaurant in Perth's entertainment district a few weeks after my discovery. Expecting my news to come as a shock, I put it to him as a question, hoping to soften the blow: *Did you know your grandfather was beaten up by eight men?*

Dad speared an arancini ball with his fork, popped it into his mouth and chewed slowly. *Afterwards, he went round to each of their houses and beat them up,* he said.

James Te Teira went around and beat them up after they had beaten him up? I asked.

Dad nodded. Reached for another arancini ball. *Yeah.*

But why did they beat him up in the first place? The first newspaper article I had found online didn't say.

Dad shrugged. *Probably sleeping with all their wives.*

Stories upon stories, circles upon circles. Around and around we go, building our histories on half-truths and unspoken words, slowly shaping a past that portrayed us as victors, the good guys, the maltreated. We never stop to wonder what it might mean for those who'll come later, those who'll grow up on unsteady ground, unable to confidently take their next step.

One of my family members has said this is not my story to tell. When I sent her a version of this essay, she rang and began listing all the ways I'd got it wrong. I only remember a few things she said. You'll have to forgive me; I was sobbing for most of it, the kind of crying where you can't seem to find enough breath to get your words out. *You haven't written it in a te ao Māori framework*, she said. I shouldn't have begun a story by mentioning the dead. She wanted to go through the essay line-by-line so she could point out every part she had an issue with.

I was caught in an artillery bombardment, each accusation she lobbed my way sending sprays of dirt skywards and catching my hair, shoulders, legs. I held out for about half an hour, doing my best to explain my point of view even when it was obvious she wasn't listening, but eventually—because I'm a Walker, because we attack when our backs are against the wall—I told her to fuck off and hung up.

I wish I'd managed to explain how I can't separate my life from those of my father, my grandfather, my great-grandfather, how our pasts are overlapping and tangled like an impossibly snarled wire. I inherited what happened to them the moment I came into this world. Their lives were the nutrients that fed me as I grew. The things they left unsaid shook the earth beneath my feet.

NATIVE DIVORCE

A DANNEVIRKE CASE

In the Supreme Court at Palmerston North yesterday, before the Chief Justice, Sir Michael Myers, Tame Moana Karaitiana (Mr P.W. Dorrington), of Makirikiri, cited adultery as the grounds for his application for divorce from Emere Piriha Karaitiana, whom he married at Carterton on March 7, 1929. The issue of the marriage was two children. Petitioner cited James Walker as co-respondent. ... This week he discovered respondent had a child born in February or March 1934, and that she was still living with Walker.

Henare Puke, living next door to Mrs Karaitiana, said her latest child was named Barry Walker. Co-respondent and respondent were living together as man and wife ...

A decree nisi was granted ...[5]

There's a kernel of truth in the story Dad told me when I asked why eight men had beaten James Te Teira. It *was* because of somebody's wife. Not multiple wives, though, just one: Emere, the woman who would become my great-grandmother.

Everyone knew they were seeing each other, apparently. A neighbour—one of the men who'd taken part in the assault—said James Te Teira had once come to his house while Emere was visiting and refused to leave. In the end, the neighbour had had to grab him by his coat and drag him out. Emere's husband had arrived as this was happening and had taken one of his children and walked out to the road. James Te Teira had followed her husband, threatening to beat up both him and the neighbour.[6]

Another time, James Te Teira drank too much, entered the same neighbour's house, and passed out on his couch. After being shaken awake, James Te Teira said he'd go to Emere's house. The neighbour followed and tried to get him to leave, but James Te Teira told him to mind his own business. As he turned to go, the neighbour overheard James Te Teira speaking to Emere's husband. 'Suppose I tell you why I love your wife', he'd said.[7]

Emere's mātua whāngai dropped by one evening and discovered James Te Teira standing at Emere's bedroom door while she lay in bed. Emere's husband was nowhere to be seen. When Emere's mother objected to him being there, James Te Teira said he wasn't afraid of anybody and if he wanted a woman, married or single, he would have her.[8]

The people at Mākirikiri tried to expel him, a body rejecting a foreign object, seeing him as a threat to the health of their community. But James Te Teira was nothing if not persistent. He dug in and stuck it out, using the passage of time to his advantage. Everyone around him knew what he'd done, what type of person he was. They may have held their tongues out of respect for his children and mokopuna, who spent their school lunchtimes playing with the descendants of the men who'd beaten James Te Teira, but I doubt they ever forgot. A collective silence simply settled over it all.

Dad and I contemplate Gamps's headstone. *It's weird*, I say. *I spent most of my life being afraid of Gamps, but now I just feel sorry for him.*

Two and a half years after his tangihanga, we have returned to Dannevirke for Gamps's hura kōhatu. Most families give it a single year before unveiling a headstone, but our family has never really conformed to tradition.

Recently painted in white, Gamps's headstone shines like a beacon in the midday sun. Two small boulders, carted in from the coast to show Gamps's love for the sea, stand guard on either side. They are dotted with fossilised shells, which give them a puffy, cloud-like quality. His plaque is black, the inscription gold:

BARRY WALKER
30 Jan 1934 – 6 Aug 2017
'He aroha ki te moana,
tutaki atu ai'

Beside Gamps, James and Emere's headstone looks worn. Their names are difficult to read thanks to the calcium calling cards left by years of rain. Old lichen, dried and mustard yellow, covers the concrete base.

A few months ago while searching an audiovisual archive, I found a silent black-and-white film that had been shot at Gamps's primary school. *Teachers' refresher course*, the title frame read. *Dannevirke South School. June 1945. Class activity and group work with forms I and II.*

The film showed children doing P.E. drills. They are dressed in black shorts, the boys shirtless, girls in white blouses. Lined up, they skip on the spot and clap in time. Bent forward, hands on knees, their classmates leapfrog over them.

Gamps makes an appearance in a line of kids at two minutes and 33 seconds. A boy directs two others out of the line and Gamps steps out from behind some girls to get a better look. His hair is long on top, short on the sides. He squints in the sun. His hand is clenched down by his thigh. He reaches up and scratches the side of his mouth. Pulls on his nose.

There's no way Gamps wouldn't have known, I say, staring down at Emere and James Te Teira's headstone. *Someone would have said something to him.*

He probably would've been fighting all the time, says Dad. *No way your grandfather would've let anyone speak badly of his father.*

I remember how protective I'd felt towards the little boy when he scratched his face and I'd seen a plaster on his index finger, white against his skin. I had wanted to reach through the screen and pick him up, to clutch him to me and escape into another life.

Beyond the urupā, the paddocks are parched, fragile and paper-thin. Off in the distance, Ruahine's forested slopes are almost black against the cloudless sky. They're the only thing standing between us and oblivion—without the ranges tying them down, the soil, trees and grass will lift off, slowly dissipating into thin air.

I always forget how beautiful it is out here, I say to Dad, taking in the sight.

Yup, he agrees. *Māori always give their dead the best seats in the house.*

I've never seen it this dry, though. It's starting to look like WA.

I pat one of the boulders framing Gamps's headstone while Dad strokes the other. We turn and make our way back to the car as the grass, crisp from months without rain, crunches beneath our shoes.

NB: *Where necessary, the quoted records have been changed so people are referred to using the names by which they are most commonly known.*

Notes
1. *Hawkes Bay Today*, 8 August 2017.
2. *Manawatu Daily Times*, 6 May 1933, p. 8.
3. *Manawatu Daily Times*, 5 May 1933, p. 8.
4. *Dannevirke Evening News*, 4 May 1933, p. 5.
5. *Dannevirke Evening News*, 9 February 1935, p. 2.
6. *Manawatu Daily Times*, 6 May 1933, p. 8.
7. Ibid.
8. *Manawatu Daily Times*, 5 May 1933, p. 8.
9. J. Peacock, 'Teachers' refresher course, Dannevirke South School, June 1945', Ngā Taonga Sound and Vision, F1511.

HANNAH AUGUST

Response to a Restructure

> What is most distinctive, and perhaps distinctively valuable, about what universities do is precisely what cannot be captured by the metrics societies increasingly use to measure value.
>
> <div align="right">Stefan Collini, <i>Speaking of Universities</i></div>

Towards the end of 2023, humanities scholars at my university were sent a document that outlined what our value to the institution was—or more precisely, what it should be and was not. Construing value in monetary terms, the document announced which disciplines were failing to contribute satisfactorily to the annual income of the university. It set out, in precise dollar amounts, how far each discipline was from achieving the 'target contribution' someone had decreed it should be able to offer to the university's total revenue. And then—predictably—the document proposed that the way to make financially disappointing disciplines return better value (for money) was to reduce their operating costs by cutting the number of staff who taught and researched within those disciplines: Chinese, Japanese, Spanish, Classics, History, Philosophy, Writing Studies, my own discipline of English Literature. It suggested which roles should go in order to meet the required savings targets, listing them by job title. The number of staff in the disciplines targeted was already small, so it was easy, in most cases, to guess which person's name sat behind each job title. But the document did not use our names. For its purposes we were not people, just dollar amounts representing the salary that might be returned to the university's coffers once we no longer worked there.

    We were invited to offer feedback on the document, knowing that it was unlikely this would alter the course of action it outlined. We tried, as so many had done before us at other times and in other universities, to explain why the scale of the proposed cuts would prevent us from maintaining credible disciplinary expertise. We attempted to stay conscious of the financial imperative and pointed out that fewer staff meant fewer courses on offer, which meant that our degree programmes would be less appealing to potential students, which meant that our income from student fees would go down, which meant that the revenue issues would not, in fact, go away. We tried to understand how providing us with offices could cost more and more money every year, and to get our heads around the formulae that were used to calculate space costs and real estate depreciation. We suggested other ways of saving money, worrying secretly that these would diminish our ability to do the things that defined us as scholars: to think and read and write and talk with students. We were not mathematicians, but we set aside words and tried to focus on numbers. When we did use words, we chose them carefully—nothing too emotive, a paucity of adverbs and adjectives. We wanted to be taken seriously, to be seen as contributing constructively to a possible alternative approach—after all, the people who read our feedback were the people who would decide whether we kept our jobs. We did not mention our anger, or our hurt, or our bewilderment at the scale and suddenness of the budget deficit that now had to be addressed by job cuts when we had watched shiny new multi-million-dollar buildings go up across the quad. We did not try—or we did not try very hard—to insist on a different understanding of our value.

While our feedback was reviewed, I re-read a book that I had first read ten years ago, shortly after finishing my PhD. *Stoner* is a 1965 novel by the American writer and scholar, John Williams. Its protagonist, William Stoner, is an only child from Missouri whose parents are farmers. They are poor, taciturn, prematurely aged by their battle with the land. Stoner's father believes that his son might have more success with the family farm if exposed to 'new ideas, ways of doing things', and sends him off to the University of Missouri to study for a bachelor's degree in the College of Agriculture. But in 1910, the disciplinary boundary between the arts and the sciences is still porous, and in his second year Stoner is required to take a compulsory survey course in English literature.

In a class on Shakespeare's sonnets, something happens to dull, diligent Stoner. The man teaching the class recites a sonnet—number 73—and then asks Stoner for his views on the poem: 'What does [Shakespeare] say to you, Mr Stoner? What does his sonnet mean?' Stoner has no answer. But in that moment he undergoes a transformation. The sonnet, and the instructor's probing questions about it, unlock something within him. He experiences a heightened sensory awareness of the world around him—the feel of the classroom's wooden floor beneath his feet, the rasping sound of his shoes as he walks across it, the sight of the leafless winter trees outside the teaching building. He goes home and changes his degree to a Bachelor of Arts, majoring in English Literature, and two years later, the instructor who precipitated this shift of focus will diagnose its cause: '"It's love, Mr Stoner," Sloane said cheerfully. "You are in love. It's as simple as that."'

Stoner's love of literature and learning will propel him through a life that is, on a number of fronts, difficult and unhappy. Like all great love affairs, it brings both pleasure and pain. Having progressed to PhD study in English Literature, he makes friends with a fellow graduate student; this friend dies in action in World War I. He initially shares his love of reading and thinking with his young daughter; noticing this, his jealous wife drives a wedge between them. His role as an assistant professor in the University of Missouri's English Department throws him into the path of his soulmate; the vindictiveness of a colleague removes her from his life. Yet in the novel's concluding scene, as Stoner lies on his deathbed, he reflects: 'He was himself, and he knew what he had been.' This 'sense of his own identity' comes to him just before he reaches out to the table of books by his bedside and grasps the book that he himself had written years before. 'He did not have the illusion that he would find himself there, in that fading print; and yet, he knew, a small part of him that he could not deny *was* there, and would be there.' In the modulation of tenses—*was, had been, would be*—Williams captures part of what books can achieve. They shape the identity of those who read them, and they preserve, for posterity, part of the identity of those who write them. To read deeply and widely is both to know more of others, and to better know ourselves.

I first read *Stoner* in my late twenties, at a time when—disillusioned by the poverty and loneliness of my final year of PhD study—I am trying to convince myself that I have fallen out of love with books, and that a career in academia is no longer something I want. I remember the novel as one that mirrored my state of mind and affirmed the meaninglessness of researching and teaching in a university. Re-reading it ten years later, I am surprised to find that this is not what it does at all. Williams tricks the reader: a prefatory chapter announces that Stoner achieved little of note, that 'few students remembered him with any sharpness after they had taken his courses', and that 'Stoner's colleagues ... held him in no particular esteem when he was alive.' And then the novel goes on to show, in devastating detail, why judging someone simply by their professional achievements distorts and devalues the shape of their life. It acknowledges that Stoner is more than the (literal) sum of his scholarly career—and also that this career has been stymied by domestic, institutional and societal pressures over which he has little control. In the times when he is freed from these pressures, he teaches well, infusing his lectures with the emotion that fired him as an undergraduate:

> The love of literature, of language, of the mystery of the mind and heart showing themselves in the minute, strange, and unexpected combinations of letters and words, in the blackest and coldest print—the love which he had hidden as if it were illicit and dangerous, he began to display, tentatively at first, and then boldly, and then proudly.

In the years since I rediscovered my own love of literature and language and, soon after, was hired to teach English Literature in a New Zealand university, I, too, have often hidden this love away. Not in the encounters I have facilitated between students and the 'minute, strange, and unexpected combinations of letters and words' previously opaque to them. Rather, I have done so every time I have proclaimed the discipline of English as one that has value because it trains students to think critically, to communicate more clearly, to be more aware of the world around them. I have done so when parroting statistics that demonstrate it is valuable because it increases graduates' earning capacity. It is; it does. It does all these things. But after I have cried at Stoner's death, and gone back to a campus largely empty of students and colleagues, where the shelves of the library are bare because the books have been moved into storage for a renovation no longer deemed financially justifiable, where a gardener ensures that the lawns and flower-beds in front of the senior leadership team's offices remain immaculate, I no longer want to talk this way. I no longer want to reduce the study of 'the mystery of the mind and heart' to a list of utilitarian co-benefits, because to do so is to help construct the university as a place inimical to love.

To defend humanities disciplines using the language of instrumentalism *does not work*. Such defences have been mounted with regularity over the past decades, in Aotearoa and elsewhere, as cyclical periods of restructures and redundancies become part of business-as-usual at universities shaped by neoliberal values. These defences fail because we make them in the language of corporate management rather than our own; they fail because we accept the managers' definition of value, rather than insisting on the validity of other definitions and other ways of understanding worth.

★

Nested among the Oxford English Dictionary's twenty-one usages for the noun 'value' is this one:

> **value** (n.), sense I.5.f.
> Chiefly *Linguistics* and *Semiotics*. The place or function of a sign within a system of signs from which it derives its meaning.

I first encountered this definition—which originates in the writings of the structuralist thinker Ferdinand de Saussure—in an Honours course I took at the University of Otago in 2005. It was the type of course English Literature students at New Zealand universities no longer have the opportunity to take, a full-year theory course, co-taught by scholars in the Classics and English departments. Its aim was to introduce us to what people had thought, from the time of Plato to the time of Derrida, about what literature was and what it could do. Because I was twenty-one and it was a different time I was unconcerned by the fact that those people were predominantly White, and male, and from Western centres of culture. I was in love with the process of connection, with mapping the way every critic built on the work of their predecessors—even if only to argue against it—creating a centuries-old chain of knowledge that I was beginning to think I, too, might want to be a part of. The course showed me a world where the things I loved and cared about were important, often vitally so, where to read and think and deploy carefully chosen language to articulate your thoughts were activities worth doing.

Saussure featured on the course not because he was a literary theorist, but because he is the father of semiotics. Semiotics is important in the history of twentieth-century literary theory because it (and Saussure in particular) places pressure on the meanings of words, their connection to—and therefore possible disconnection from—the thing they signify. It is Saussure who points out that the signifier (a word) has only an arbitrary connection with its signified (its meaning), and also that this meaning is separate from its value. Value, for Saussure, is a part of meaning, but it is the part that is defined by a word's relationship *with other words*, by being a word that other words are not. 'Language is a system of interdependent terms in which the value of each term results solely from the simultaneous presence of the others', he says. Saussure's conception of language systems acknowledges that words have a value that derives from their place in a community. In using this term, 'community', he opposes it to the individual, who 'by himself ... is incapable of fixing a single value.' Value cannot inhere in an individual alone, only in the interrelation of that individual with others. It is the community that gives value to its members.

As my colleagues and I write carefully crafted responses to the restructure proposal in which we argue that the loss of a particular individual or a particular discipline will leave the university weaker overall, Saussure's definition of value offers itself up as a reminder that words can have multiple meanings. Because those meanings can be figurative as well as literal, it also offers an alternative way of thinking about the institution the proposal claims to want to save. A *university* is a system of interdependent terms (individual scholars, disciplines) in which the value of each term results solely from the simultaneous presence of others. Value inheres not in the individual, but in the community.

In the 2020 New Zealand Education and Training Act, the 'community' is presented as distinct from the university: 'a university is characterised by a wide diversity of teaching and research, especially at a higher level, that maintains, advances, disseminates, and assists the application of knowledge, develops intellectual independence, and promotes community learning.' What happens within the university benefits the wider community outside the university. But a university is itself a community: a community of scholars and students and the people who support them to do what a university first and foremost exists to do, which is to maintain and advance knowledge through 'a wide diversity of teaching and research'. And as Saussure points out, everyone in the community has value based on their connection to others in the community. A scholar has value because they know something that others do not, but this value is diminished if they cannot share this knowledge with students or colleagues. A scholar of seventeenth-century English literature is only an expert if there are other members of her department who have expertise in other areas: the fewer members of a department, the less capacity for a scholar to define herself against what others do, and the more her expertise is dulled and diluted as she is asked to teach courses once the remit of departed colleagues. Librarians have value in the service relationship they have with those who need information; the work done by scholars and students is shaped by encounters with librarians. English Literature has value because it is not Physics and also because it is not Art History—each discipline is defined not just by its sphere of enquiry and the approaches to understanding that it requires, but the fact that these are distinct from those of other disciplines *with whom they co-exist*. The fewer disciplines supported within the university, the less distinct and valuable those that remain become, and the university becomes a place no longer characterised by a 'wide diversity' of teaching and research, but by homogeneity and narrowed horizons.

In this understanding of value, the university is a tessellation of interconnected parts, all of which derive their individual worth from their connection to other parts of the system. This is what a university restructure never acknowledges, instead insisting on individuals and programmes as separate entities, which can be excised from the whole in order to redistribute their reclaimed value, which is always defined—implicitly or explicitly—in monetary terms. When I worked briefly in the public sector before taking up my lectureship, I told my colleagues I was worried about the projects I would leave incomplete by moving on. They scoffed. 'Leaving the public sector is like taking your hand out of a basin of water,' said one—you can't even see the space you once filled. Leaving a university is different. The value of the former staff member is changed as their years of training and experience go to waste, but so too is the value of the parts that remain, which can no longer derive meaning from departed members of staff or disestablished disciplines. The community, and its purpose, are devalued.

The restructures and programmes of redundancies that have plagued Aotearoa's universities in recent years are destroying the idea of the university as a community, but so too are trends that work against the idea that it is the 'simultaneous *presence* of others' that constructs mutual value. In my university, it is a core part of the business model that research and education do not require presence, 'the state of being with or in the same place as a 'person or thing' ('presence (n.), sense 1.a')—and that instead these things can be entirely mediated by screens. Distance teaching democratises higher education, it enables those who cannot attend scheduled lectures and tutorials to learn despite this, it allows students to achieve their goals without altering their living circumstances. At the same time, it negates a key tenet of tikanga Māori, the importance of meeting kanohi ki te kanohi or face-to-face—not in glitch-riven Zoom rooms, but in the same physical space, where breath can be shared. It also seems to exacerbate students' mental health problems, and it removes the aspect of teaching that gives scholars a sense of purpose: the instantaneous feedback that comes in the form of a room full of straightened shoulders, focused attention, engaged questioning. It is harder to share love on a screen.

A university is a physical community, one that is constituted by people being in the same place, at the same time, as other people. It is the scholars who converse in corridors and the students who cross a quad on their way to lectures. It is the academically conscientious who set up home in the library or the lab, and the librarians and technicians who make them welcome. It is the creatively curious who inhabit the drama department, and the cleaners who vacuum up the crumbs of their rejected ideas. It is the slackers and the swots, the student politicians and the sports stars. It is a petri dish of people, jostling against one another to grow a culture. The wasteland of my university campus is not a sign that the university has simply been displaced into the siloed spaces of its staff and students' digital devices. It is a sign that the community is dying. Locked office doors bear the names of staff who no longer come onto campus to work, because nothing about their job requires them to interact with other members of the university community in the same physical environment. The students catch the scent of decay and disaffection, and choose to study from home rather than enrol in the dwindling number of face-to-face classes on offer. The university has become a place where individuals have begun to forget that their value exists in the fact that they are part of a community.

★

The Shakespearean sonnet that Stoner's instructor recites to his class is about the inexorable advance of death. The speaker describes himself as past his prime: he has reached 'That time of year …/ When yellow leaves, or none, or few do hang/ Upon those boughs which shake against the cold.' Doubling down on the imagery of moribundity, he likens himself to the fading light of the moments after sunset, to the embers of a dying fire (built on 'the ashes of … youth'). Yet as with so many of Shakespeare's sonnets, this is not the whole story. In the couplet with which the poem concludes, its subject speaks directly to the sonnet's addressee, the observer of the speaker's decrepitude. It is the speaker's proximity to death, says the couplet, that acts as a catalyst for love.

> This thou perceiv'st, which makes thy love more strong,
> To love that well, which thou must leave ere long.

Over three centuries later, Dylan Thomas will offer an alternative emotion as the appropriate response to mortality, and urge his father to 'Rage, rage, against the dying of the light.' Both poems assume an inevitable death for the thing that is loved, be it a beloved or life itself. When it comes to the idea of the university as a community, to the status of the humanities as important scholarly disciplines, and to the place of English literature as one of these, I am not yet willing to accept this inevitability.

Convention says you cannot respond to a restructure proposal by quoting poetry. It is not the done thing to invoke the specialist knowledge that the proposal aims to diminish, to counter 'facts' and figures by deploying the tools of literary analysis and composition. In the third-year feminist literature course that I teach, my students are still excited to read Audre Lorde's 1983 pronouncement that the master's tools will never dismantle the master's house. To respond to the reductive conception of value that underpins the documents which determine the fates of individual scholars, disciplines, communities, *in the same language* is to accept that the master's tools are the only ones there are. To acknowledge instead that the toolkit of language is 'incorrigibly plural' is to insist on a different type of value. 'I peel and portion / A tangerine and spit the pips and feel / The drunkenness of things being various,' writes Louis MacNeice. To use the language of poetry, of analogy and metaphor and symbolism, is to speak the university as a place where 'the drunkenness of things being various' is a cause for celebration, not concern.

In Shakespeare's *Measure for Measure*, the character of Isabella pleads with the managerial duke's deputy, Angelo, for a reprieve of her brother's death sentence. Angelo demurs: 'He's sentenced; 'tis too late.' And Isabella responds: 'Too late? Why, no, I that do speak a word / May call it again.' The slippery sentence construction contains the possibility that a word can be retracted or 'recalled', but also that it can be spoken again with a different meaning, 'called' something else. An alternative signification can be summoned into being, and an execution forestalled. Speech can be performative, can create something out of nothing, can cast things in a different light—one that can be left to flicker and die or one that can be sustained and nurtured, depending, perhaps, on the weight we choose to give to love.

This essay's epigraph comes from a book by the British intellectual historian, Stefan Collini, who has written extensively about the changed nature of universities since the 1980s. He, too, points to the power of language to be performative:

> Words are not a kind of decorative wrapping paper in which meaning is delivered, with the implication that they could be stripped away, or others used in their stead, without making any difference to the 'real' content. Concepts colonize our minds and we become used to thinking about ourselves and our world in their terms[.]

In this country where colonisation is more than a metaphor, the concept that has come to dominate the mental landscape of those who think about and work in universities is value, narrowly defined in economic—or, at best, instrumental—terms. Before I or my colleagues are made redundant because our discipline is deemed to be of insufficient value and our own value to inhere solely in the redistributive potential of our salaries, I wanted to consider how we might take this word and 'call it again', to give it a different meaning using, as Collini puts it, 'a vocabulary appropriate to the activities being discussed.' That is, a vocabulary that acknowledges that fiction and poetry and drama and philosophy and the tools of literary composition and critique can offer different conceptions of the value of the university community and its members, of humanities disciplines such as English Literature, of words, and of love.

Works cited

Stefan Collini, *Speaking of Universities* (Verso, 2017).
Audre Lorde, 'The master's tools will never dismantle the master's house', in *The Master's Tools Will Never Dismantle the Master's House* (Penguin, 2018).
Louis MacNeice, 'Snow' in *The Collected Poems of Louis MacNeice* (Oxford UP, 1967).
Ferdinand de Saussure, *Course in General Linguistics*, eds Charles Bally & Albert Sechehaye, with Albert Reidlinger; trans. Wade Baskin (Owen, 1974).
William Shakespeare, *Measure for Measure*, ed. J.M. Nosworthy (Penguin, 2015).
—'Sonnet 73', in *Shakespeare's Sonnets*, ed. Katherine Duncan-Jones (The Arden Shakespeare, 2005).
Dylan Thomas, 'Do not go gentle into that good night', in *The Collected Poems of Dylan Thomas* (New Directions Publishing Corporation, 1957).
John Williams, *Stoner* (Vintage, 2012).
Definitions and etymological information from the Oxford English Dictionary, online version.

ELESE DOWDEN

aye i

it's as if the pigeon doesn't move at all
& only the wings & the pigeon steady
is this how they designed drones to go
with this splendid economy of flight
a helicopter like a mynah with a single
overhead wing flying string tv antenna
ahead red brick of old fires slim graffiti
up top air vents whirring and becoming
seriouser with each deft rotation silver
see it comes from nowhere this nothing
a nobody's home decision-making unit
conspired by a much lesser gendarmerie
no subject to invade the paddling pool
(a collectivity forms a protective unit)
the anti-somersault hegemony worser
than a thought that counts a separation
between only two whereas the rest are
multiple & by training a binary for this
might we find a map of western mind
a glass for the holy spirit, pink-nosed
poised & writing to think about the sky

PERENA QUINLIVAN

Long Distance

Spring attends you but it brings no joy.
From the boulevard below your apartment
raucous trams and fragrant blossoms
scratch your senses like coarse wool.

Here, I lust for ridged certainty in the
Pacific's soup lumbering autumn.
You appear on the screen,
dazzling, innocent, my Milky Way.

Trying to be there, yet being here,
a baffled silence surfaces
from the poor connection. How will this end
without the nearness of you?

JANET NEWMAN

Kukutauaki

Kukutauaki, you stick
in my white throat like dry Weetbix.
Tongue-tied, I try to sound a simpler sign,
clipped, colonial, easy to sup through teeth
as milk from a cow's teat.

I occupy your vowels with my proper
pronunciation, my English education,
cuckold kuku, tar and tacky feather tauaki,
lay my invasive egg in your nest,
hatch an intruder's name in my throat.

It comes out square and hard,
inhabits the ear, the ground, resists
your flow with my charted line,
sucks you dry, Kukutauaki Stream,
significant tribal boundary drained of meaning.

KEITH NUNES

Pendulum

The grandfather has spent the entire Sunday treading around his home as though he were in a minefield. Family are coming and going, debating floral arrangements, a bridesmaid's bitchiness and the fast-approaching new millennium.

Grandfather is now fiddling with his clock in the basement, a safe space. This morning he made the mistake of offering advice on the seating plan for the reception. Later he stumbled upon his grandson, the groom, and gave him an ancient condom. The look on the kid's face floored him, then they laughed together.

He'll wait to be summoned, knowing then that his emotional safety would be guaranteed.

How many marriages have been staged in the back garden over the forty years he and his wife have lived here? How many ended in divorce? Too many.

His hearing is still impeccable so he picks up via the slim basement windows what's going on outside. When he hears the bride telling her sister she's having grave doubts he wants to rush outside and comfort her, in the knowledge that his grandson is a good man in the making, and has a bright future in pharmaceuticals. But that's not it.

The bride has been given some information about her intended's family background, about the groom's grandfather and his behaviour in the war. The grandfather feels faint, sits quickly on the concrete floor and begins to shake his head like a pendulum, like the Edgar Allan Poe pendulum.

ISABEL HAARHAUS

Dog Days

It was my job to make Ben breakfast. He liked wheat biscuits with warm milk and sugar, and I enjoyed preparing it for him, taking time to arrange a pattern in the big enamel bowl, tormenting him with my fussing around.

He was part Boxer and part Dalmatian, a big, bounding dog that slobbered and scratched and sniffed at adult crotches. His claws were black and hoary and too long and he made a mess of everything, always getting into trouble with our father, who beat him with a rolled-up newspaper. The theory was that the tightly rolled paper stick didn't hurt, just shocked him with the loud thwack. But when I tried it on myself I knew they were lying, the angry welts on my arm glaring accusingly.

I can't remember a time before Ben but do remember thinking that I understood why we had to take him to live with another family just over the border. Our village, our townhouse, our lives in Holland were too small for Ben, who wanted to jump and sprint and chase. He quivered and whined with all the things he wanted to do, our father told us. With us he was pent up and frustrated, our babysitter said. And we knew that the biggest run he got was when, on our way back from visiting family in Germany, our father shoved him out of the van to run along behind us for the last straight stretch of road.

He would sprint stumblingly along, his skinny barrel torso twisted and his face strained, black eyes hectic and pleading, implicating my brother and me stuck mortified behind the window. But what could we do? We were children of the 70s in the back of a VW combi van, partitioned off from our parents in the front cabin, guiltily watching our dog race along the Autobahn, his tongue lolling in the wind, his skinny legs buckling on the thin grass verge. We were in no position to help him.

Sometimes our mother took Ben along the narrow lanes through the fields around our village and he peacefully loped along while she rode her bike. That was a picture. All flat fields with bright green grass that looked good enough to eat, gridded with skinny canals and tall pale poplars under a lilac sky.

The Friesians formed a picturesque motif with his black and white coat. A Dutch tile or biscuit-tin picture.

But most of the time he was inside bouncing off the walls with us, cowering and pining, wanting something, ready for anything.

Oh how we loved him, our naughty gorgeous Ben! We dressed him up in antique nighties and velvet waistcoats, jammed old sailor's caps and *Star Wars* masks on his head and overfed him elaborate concoctions: raw egg with brown sugar and grated coconut, *Speckpfannekuchen, boerenkool*. He was our pet.

We stayed with the Hoffmans for the weekend we gave them Ben. There were the parents and two boys around my brother's age of thirteen. The eldest grew up to become a policeman, who, when I went back to visit years later, marched me around Frankfurt to point out in fear and loathing all the places now supposedly lost to him: the 'Deutsche-Frei Zone'. 'It's all Muslim now—all the signs, all the food,' policeman Rolf complained, waving his soft bluish hands at the döner kebab and falafel shops.

'And look at the women. All covered up in those ridiculous sheets.' He still spoke the way he had as a child, in a honking monotone that pushed up and out from his chest as if automated. But his movements were jaunty and each time we passed a group of murmuring men sitting around smoking hookah they turned, distracted (as I was) by Rolf's weirdly mannered gait.

Those were the days of *Ausländer Raus* (Foreigners Out) scrawled across the walls in West Germany, and Rolf wanted me to agree with him that Germany was ruined. 'First these filthy *Ausländer* and now the *Ossis* coming in from East Germany too. We're losing everything again.' Of course I didn't agree with anything he was saying. By then I was a hippy living in New Zealand and, coming from an island in the South Pacific, I didn't know or care about the European xenophobic sense of entitlement to *Lebensraum* and anyway, Rolf would always be the guy whose family took my dog.

I hadn't forgotten that the weekend we stayed at the Hoffmans' Rolf was also the boy who tripped up his younger brother on purpose when his parents weren't looking, gestured obscenities behind his father's back before obsequiously flattering him to his face, and held the dog biscuits just out of Ben's reach. I didn't like the way he yanked at Ben's lead when we took him on the inaugural walk around the property. Ben wasn't a barker but when he smelt the horses he went off and I remember hoping then and there that the parents decided against taking him. But instead the mother, Heike, just launched into part one of what presented like a rehearsed training regime, firmly holding Ben's jaw together and telling him, *Nein!*, while her eldest tugged tightly and with relish at that new lead.

Heike was tall, tanned and Amazonian with bleached cropped hair tinted reddish brown on the ends, bright blue eyes, glittering jewellery and massive white American teeth. She laughed heartily from her taut stomach, and even inside strode around with purpose in black riding boots and jodhpurs. She smelt of leather and peppermint and was the very opposite of our mother, who wafted through life in layered muslin and off-the-shoulder jumpers threaded with lurex, her bare or sandalled feet never quite on the ground. Our mother was warm and soft; her hands smelt of nutmeg and her voice was a faraway, soporific song. Heike was the strident muscled trunk to her maidenhair fern.

Where our mother was enigmatic—*poetic*—Heike, from her tall, sturdy vantage, clocked everything and everyone, shouted plans and delegated, organised and oversaw. She was a bullet-pointed list to our mother's slant rhyme. 'Rolf, have you turned the hay in the stables? Rudiger, what sort of state is your room? Heinrich, where did you leave my riding crop? Children, what time do you usually take your lunch?' My brother and I weren't used to such supervision and confounded Heike with our seeming (insolent?) inability to follow orders and stick to the plan. Instead, we wandered off track and out of sight, easily distracted.

It was winter the weekend we gave Ben away and after arriving at the Hoffmans' late at night we woke early to the soothing shock of a world muffled white by heavy snowfall. Ben and my brother and I were in sync (as usual) and didn't speak as we got ourselves together to sweep around the house, taking stock while finding the way out. In the kitchen a fire still smouldered, but the house was cold with dark wood-panelled walls, high steel casement windows and big rounded terracotta floor tiles covered in Persian rugs. On the walls hung watercoloured botanical etchings, elaborately framed black and white photographs of thoroughbred horses, and paintings of grim-looking ancestors whose eyes followed us around. The only sounds were a ticking clock, Ben's claws clacking on the tiles and our own beating hearts.

As was our habit, we rummaged as we slid around, expertly opening drawers and cupboards without saying a word, and before we even got outside we had already taken a dusty gold wristwatch, a silver pen and a single coral earring. The earring reminded me of the necklaces my mother wore, and of the salt and spices of which her soft brown neck smelt.

Outside our blue breath made little twisting ghosts against the pale world and Ben—still *our* Ben—silhouetted against the blank page of the Hoffmans' front lawn, was briefly a perfect platonic drawing of a 'dog'. For a moment it felt like it was just the three of us in the world. Then a few wintering cranes beat slowly across the scratchy grey sky.

I don't remember much else about that day, other than watching Ben strain at the short lead when we toured the grounds and Heike sparkling in the cold air as she held court in a barking voice. The horses would have been beautiful, of course, but were almost invisible to us in their thick felted wool covers behind high glossy stable doors, only their names accessible, engraved on shiny copper plates: Borgia, Amadeus, Mahler.

But the night was one to remember.

After a very long dinner at which we children had been ordered to stay— why?—someone, probably Heike, suggested we all have a sauna.

'But first we will roll naked in the snow to optimise the health benefits.' This was Heike's little husband Heinrich at last, and the only topic on which I remember him speaking. Mostly he just busied himself in the shadows, ridiculously dressed in a three-piece suit, pulling on his pointed silvery beard and practising an ironic inward look, as if he were pondering some riveting, insightful idea.

Other than checking whether the adults wanted their wine or schnapps topped up and reacting to Heike's imperatives, he didn't speak at all until he got on to the topic of the therapeutic benefits of extreme temperature exposure, the science of which aroused him into such a passion that his face blazed, white spittle flew from his flabby mouth and his stubby fingers stabbed into the candlelit night. It was as if a dormant garden gnome had become animated and we children were struck, then quickly repelled.

But we all did it. We all went into our respective bedrooms, stripped off, met again in the front hall as per Heike's instructions, ran into the black and white front garden and rolled around naked in the new snow. Then—now following Heinrich's instructions—we ran into the sauna, excitedly frightened at the sharp, unusual sensations, the shards stabbing in and out of our skin that felt too much alive but sort of dead too. 'It's good for you!' Heinrich had shouted in the garden. 'It keeps cancer at arm's length!' Naked, he looked even older than he did in his suit. To my brother and I he was ancient and fictional and we wished he would return to his inaudible corner, grovelling around silently behind his silvery Herculean wife.

My little plump nine-year-old body, still olive from the Mediterranean sun, patched with red from ice burns, pulsing and stinging in the dark, felt unusually conspicuous. The adults' eyes were unfocused and shiny from the alcohol they'd been drinking, their nipples disturbingly erect and obscenely red. We were used to naked adults in the 1970s. I had seen all my friends' parents' bodies, and in the summer on our boat everyone lolled about in the leathery nude.

But that night, maybe because of the electrifying temperature shocks, we were all too raw, like live wires about to ignite then explode. When we touched someone in that unlikely tumble, we stung and thrilled and shrieked while Ben whimpered outside, leaping against the door with his too-long black claws (Heike would clip those, I knew), his face the nightmarish flash of a last-ditch attempt framed by the window.

Inside the sauna we children outnumbered the adults and our father felt even further away than usual. When we calmed down and then totally mellowed out with the heat, incrementally reduced to a sort of stupor by each eucalyptus hiss, our little bodies imprinted by the cedar benches on which we slouched, we noticed that our father was weirdly familiar with Heike. They were talking about things we had never heard him talk about to our mother: horse stuff, financial stuff, business stuff. They seemed to know a lot of people we had never met. They were verbose and wholehearted, enthusiastically interrupting each other, even finishing off each other's sentences. Their energetic intonation was entirely incongruous with the soft, hot state to which our bodies were in thrall. We had never heard our father say so much at once and listened and watched in silent horror.

By then Heinrich had resumed his subservient position, slumped with that pathetic myopic air about him, working hard to look undisturbed and fascinated by his own thoughts while his wife presided glamorously in the velvety hut. Even here she gave orders in between her communion with our father. 'Don't sit too close to the heat, Heinrich. Add another ladle of water. Inhale deeply, children, the löyly is good for your lungs.' I lied and said I'd been in a sauna lots of times and my brother didn't correct me, as was our long-established code.

'My friend has one; we do this all the time,' I drawled, trying hard to sound nonchalant. But actually I felt pretty faint and was struggling to sit up, not least intimidated by Heike's terrific, trained posture. She sat up rod straight as if her body weren't melting, as if she were riding dressage, and waved her strong hands around, captivating our father. The diamonds on her rings and around her taut tanned neck caught the flecks of light from the steaming embers, punctuating her commanding form and speech.

We were captivated by this woman, so strange and foreign to us and different to the women we knew, who were self-consciously whimsical, bending in to see the tiny spots on a creature's wings, blowing the seeds from a fragile green stem, reading Heinrich Heine while eating gooseberries. Heike was all fortitude, her body a solid silvered shield towards which our father leant, completing a sparkling field of memories and plans and lusty laughter that went on too long, causing my brother—and even the sons—and I to eyeball one another in a fleeting synergy of shared dark knowledge.

Other than that brief flash of recognition in the sauna, we didn't connect with the two boys all weekend and did our fair share of eyerolling about them too. Not least because they were so attached to, yet also so obviously scared of, their parents. Both attitudes were embarrassing anathema to us, who had long made a point of barely registering our own parents, so far away were they in their adult world of adults and adult things: couples and boats and random disappearing.

Our life and the lives of our parents were appropriately far apart, we thought, crossing only briefly at the beginnings and ends of obligatory family gatherings. Our life was with Ben and our babysitter. So spending all that time with our father and Heike and her husband the weekend we gave Ben away was unusual, and I resented the relative lack of freedom—what felt like *surveillance*—almost as much as I resented feeling increasingly held back from Ben, who, as the weekend went on, was stuck more and more at the end of that new too-short lead.

Looking back, I'm sure that from the moment those cranes beat across the sky early that first morning, Ben started pining for his unruly life with us (even if it did mean getting beaten occasionally and having to chase the car along the Autobahn). He loved us and the food I made him and wearing the gowns and coats and crown because he was our prince.

He wasn't the brightest dog I've ever met (or maybe it was just that he was untrained and lived without clear purpose or routine, leaving him bewildered and needy), but he was our Ben and we loved him, my brother and I. Our mother had loved him too in her vague, smiling way, coming in late and not keeping her word but her warm body coursing with the love she surely felt for us all: her two children and her dog, building worlds and meals at home without her, waiting for her to come in, the snow on her shoulders and the long mysterious day woven throughout her many layers of coloured fabric and wool.

Even reflecting on it today I can say that saying goodbye to Ben at the end of that snow-and-sauna-and-too-short-lead-weekend was so much harder than watching our mother's coffin being lowered into the flames just a few months earlier. What I remembered of that, and wouldn't be talked out of by anyone—not even my brother—was the sound of the crackling wood buckling under the scorching tongues of flame. I remember concentrating on that breaking sound, hoping to the bone that there weren't any bugs in that wood, like the red-spotted one our mother had pointed out to us the last time she was in our garden. I remember straining with urgent hope that the mother ladybird wasn't crawling earnestly towards her baby bugs nestled in their once-cosy knotted hollow about to be burnt to a ruthless crisp. *Let there be no creatures waiting in that wood*, I pleaded as my mother's body was incinerated in the pit of the crematorium.

But the deep strain of that strange, focused hope was nothing compared to the devastation I felt waving goodbye to Ben from the back of our van, his shivering body held tight at Heike's side. That day my heart broke. Ben. His panicked eyes darted from my face to my brother's, which, for the first time I could remember was turned away from Ben and from me, turning instead towards the front, past the back of our father's head into the future distance as we drove away from our dog.

ELIANA GRAY

Viewpoint

For shabbos
I smoke a joint
on the back step
and whisper secrets
to the moon
that's the advantage
of every holiday
being an act of
remembrance
time collapses
because it's unstable
the divine is connective tissue
a series of synonyms
that's the advantage
of synagogues being built as a circle
we're always facing each other
which is a good reminder
of what's at stake
all I'm saying is
I'm looking at the stars
and I don't see much distance
which is the advantage to a weekly reminder that we're holy
as a moss bed filtering water to the creek

TESS RITCHIE

Mother

It is always mother. The word is always mother. The thing is always mother. The reason always mother. The who always. The way she steadies herself down the leafy track is mother. That she swims on a whim is. People talk about absence as presence but absence, more specifically, is mother. At the edges and all the very ends it is mother. The album with the 'Heartbeat' track is mother, and it is called *Mother*. To will is to mother. Isn't it the dream content. The walking thigh-deep through a pool is mother. The vanilla tree is mother but not just the sweet fluffy scent I mean its navy green is mother. Its bead leaves. An open field is mother. Arriving home after the drive home is mother. To be present to insist to choose is mother. In empty rooms you will find mother. On buses. Rooftops of the parties you remember forever is mother. Holding hands is mother. Tears shed. Fears unsaid. Justice is mother. Midnight is mother. The way is mother. The where is mother. The question and the answer is mother. It is mother. Just is.

CILLA MCQUEEN

Window

The port sounds carried off by wind,
the drivers of the tall grey cranes
at screens in their control towers shift
containers in a giant Rubik's Cube.

Bees tumble among foxglove fingers.
White flowers open speckled throats.
The ochre wood-chip mountain glows.

Dazzle: the setting sun reflected on the
windscreen of a truck across the road,
new photons streaming from their source to that
windscreen, this eye, this hand that writes
until with earthly turn, unearthly
brilliance disconnects, is gone.

CADENCE CHUNG

Habits (*La Bohème*)

There's a whole host of small habits I have given myself—namely, the fringe that I keep having to smooth against the papery city wind. Magazines blow; I fold my fingers like a comb against my forehead, almost a tic. On the top floor of the Music Department I wait for the lecturer to turn his chair around. He kneels on the seat, facing back to front, leaning forward like a painting of a man. *The thing about Musetta*, he says, of my least favourite opera, *is that she's more of a woman than a woman really is. When she sings in that café—she has to break plates.* My own time in cafés has been spent with last lovers who talk of futures in London. And I can never figure out what to do with the foam on my mocha or the miscellanea on the saucer. I stir endlessly and let drinks grow cold, another bad habit. *Do you dare shrink from me?* Musetta asks, very Italian and all that. The glass-heart necklace I find myself always wearing reflects in the window of Swimsuit. I open my wrists out to find them bare, and waiting.

ATARERIA

Asks

When you ask me
To use this capability
In an empty room
You also ask me
To hold hands
Cradle salt pools
Mine and yours and all the rest
When you ask me
To define a people
Glittering seeds of Rangiātea
You pull forth guilt
From ocean depths
Create salt pools
Stretching back from me to Hine-tītama
Can I ask you
To spare a thought?
A moment, a breath
And instead ask me
Can you share?
Then feel my words
Swim my pools
And call them yours

REBECCA READER

The Sound of the Universe

Everything dates from the time Joe-Romeo came to Karma Yoga.

He had a distant brilliance about him like the stars over Lake Tekapo, and eyes full of dark energy. Most newcomers to Karma were shy about the communal 'aa-uu-um' that opened our practice, but Joe-Romeo's Om was pure bold. Long, deep and hungry, it was almost indecent. Though we'd met him only minutes before, we'd have served ourselves up for his aa-uu-um right there and then if he'd asked.

In the brief silence that followed, his hands rested palm upwards on his thighs as if they were cupping breasts on two different women. Oh Jeez, Karma Yoga was about to lose a whole heap of Zen now Joe-Romeo was in town.

In the era before Joe-Romeo, classes at Karma were as predictable as a deep breath out following a deep breath in. We warmed up, flowed fast, flowed slow, and the Sanskrit poses called by Sage drifted towards us light as dandelion seeds. There were precise moments when Sage would pause to adjust the heating, fix her hair, brush dust from her mat and lower the blinds for shavasana. And these moments were the framework that kept us moving in unison, never competing, never outshining. At times it was as if we were just one person who had climbed the stairs to the studio to climb into herself. Was there a flatness to the routine? Perhaps. But no yoga class ever needs a supernova. Then along came Joe-Romeo, acting like that was just what the studio lacked.

The studio was dark. Its one small window looked out onto a wall painted black and topped with broken glass to stop kids raiding the vape shop next door. We'd strung fairy lights along the mirrors and changed the lightbulbs, but shining that starts in a socket is no match for shining that starts in a person. When Joe-Romeo flipped his mat out in the centre of the studio and delivered his inaugural Om, we knew in an instant what the studio had been missing.

'Your Om steals the show, Joe-Romeo,' we said. Our voices hadn't been this high since 1985.

'Good lungs and a love of drama,' he said.

'We tend to be drama free, this being a yoga studio,' said Sage. Her dandelion words had a spikiness we'd never heard before, like each seed had become a tiny pin.

'Well, friends, Romans and countrymen,' said Joe-Romeo, 'you'll have to excuse my little dramas. I'm related to Shakespeare.'

'Shakespeare!'

'Joan Shakespeare, his sister.'

Sage had begun a sun salutation but stopped with her arms to the sky, as if she were deciding whether to salute the heart of the solar system or Joe-Romeo.

'Hence my name,' he said. 'Romeo, fortune's fool.'

'You're no fool, Joe-Romeo,' we said. 'Not with your Om so magnificent, so Shakespearean.'

'Did my heart love till now, ladies?' he said, looking at none of us in particular. 'But the Om is one piece of drama Shakespeare can't take credit for. It's the sound of the universe. I'm just a conduit, if you like.'

A Shakespeare *and* a conduit—right there on a mat at Karma! We liked, for sure.

'The Om means everything that ever existed,' he said, gazing at the ceiling as if he could see the stuff dreams were made of, when all we could see were loose tiles with bits of insulation hanging out.

'But can you even begin to grasp everything that ever existed?' he asked.

And we said no, Joe-Romeo, we couldn't grasp most things, let alone everything, and maybe that was why our Om had generally sounded like a dishwasher malfunctioning.

'Ladies, seriously,' he said. 'The Om ushers divinity into the room.'

Of course it did. We were serious now, because Joe-Romeo was nothing if he wasn't divine.

Joe-Romeo kept coming to class with his Bardic genes and cosmic conversations and it wasn't long before we were ditsy with dopamine and not sleeping at night. He dropped in the fact that he used to work for an astronautics company in Wisconsin designing thermal imaging systems for NASA. NASA! It made us hot just thinking about Joe-Romeo and rockets in the same thought-space. We took to waiting in our cars and playing Candy Crush until we saw him heading for the studio. Then we'd call out, 'Hey, Joe-Romeo, wait for …' our words petering out like old vapour trails across the sky.

When Joe-Romeo set his mat down every Thursday, we vied for the spot beside him, and as he moved through the flow, we inhaled his pheromones and the scent of his laundry powder. Did he do his own washing or use the laundromat—or, worst-case scenario, did a lover do it for him? We wanted no answers. Unasked questions were safer than answers that might puncture dreams, and our dream was to find Joe-Romeo's yoga pants hanging next to ours on the balcony wall of some Italian holiday home.

His yoga pants were covered in tiny Warrior 2 poses, a detail we spotted only after we'd taken in the bigger picture—a picture big enough to make our pelvic floors spasm like they hadn't in years. The Warrior 2s were small and close together around his ankles, growing larger and more imposing as they rounded his buttocks. It was like they knew that whenever Sage called for lotus pose, we would watch Joe-Romeo through our lashes, the cliff face of his chest a sheer drop amidst our own rolling hills.

'If your attention has wandered,' said Sage, 'bring yourselves back. Look for the space between your thoughts.' We did, and then we filled that space with even more Joe-Romeo.

Joe-Romeo never apologised for his Om. It ended when it chose, even if the vape shop alarm went off, or kids threw stones at the studio window. The Almighty Om was there in the room but light-years away.

'Your lungs must be huge,' we said.

'Ten litres,' he said.

'What do most people have?'

'Six maybe,' he said, casting his eyes across our rolling hills.

'Ever thought of free-diving, Joe-Romeo?'

'Red Sea. 1998 to 2002. Certified instructor,' he said.

'Wowsers!'

'Yep.'

We just couldn't get over Joe-Romeo. Relative of Shakespeare, astronautics in Wisconsin, lungs the size of watering cans, free-diving in the Red Sea. He'd been born with so many destinies we were bound to find ourselves in at least one of them. That was when we got really obsessed over who was on Joe-Romeo's radar and who was off it, and whether he was monitoring his screens on a regular basis.

Years ago, we'd have wondered whether huge lungs were something he could pass to our offspring, but we'd given up altruism the second our last kid left home. A man who rarely needed to come up for air—now, there was a thought. And that thought, like all the other thoughts we had about Joe-Romeo, made three-act farces of our sanity.

It wasn't long before we were taking Joe-Romeo to the Scran Café each week and hanging on his every word like Elizabethan groupies worshipping the bard himself. We bought Joe-Romeo espressos and pineapple upside-down cake. He gave us after-coffee mints and the beauty of his smile that widened slowly, unstoppably, like the moon coming out of eclipse.

Sage said that Joe-Romeo's mints only cost $5 a tub, as if a man with fresh breath and good financial sense was a bad thing. True reciprocity, she said, was the cornerstone of respect, but reciprocity on the cheap was a crack in that stone that would only get wider. Joe-Romeo, she said, would never be married to anything but his cash.

If we were talking personal flaws, though, we had more than enough of those—our six-litre lungs, our inferior understanding of the Om, the fact that the closest we ever got to free-diving was when we saw the Great Barrier Reef from a glass-bottom boat, and it took our breath away.

Joe-Romeo asked one of us to take a photo of him and Sage saying namaste. He wanted to promote the studio and repay the love he'd received at Karma. When the photo appeared on his social media it had been edited. Joe-Romeo was in colour and focus. Sage was an ash-grey smudge, like she'd been flash-incinerated and was a second away from collapse. Joe-Romeo said he was respecting her privacy, but Sage didn't see it that way. She said there might be plenty of room for a Joe-Romeo and the rest of us in the class, but would there be room for a Joe-Romeo and just one of us in a relationship? Could anyone get close to Joe-Romeo without catching fire? She doubted it.

One day Joe-Romeo did the whole class in sunglasses. Conjunctivitis? Cupboard door? Fight? All he said was that he didn't look as hot as normal, that this couldn't have happened at a worse time, and that it had better be gone before ten days were up. We burned to know what and why, but instead we talked arnica cream and eyedrops.

Anyone would care about their image if they were representing the world's greatest playwright. But Sage said only fools would overlook themselves for the sake of overlooking the flaws in Joe-Romeo. Weren't we tired, she said, of his stage shows, and his love of the spotlight, not to mention the stale soliloquys of his Om? She certainly was. At the next class she moved Joe-Romeo from the centre of the studio floor to a spot by the wall heater that sometimes smelt of gas.

The following Thursday, Joe-Romeo didn't come to class. Sage said she'd seen him on Monday at the bus stop with a suitcase so large it must have contained his entire life, but still, each week we hoped for the sweet sorrow of his vanishing to end. Red Sea? Wisconsin? Verona? We left him where-art-thou messages, and he left them on 'Read'. The weekly outings to the Scran Café became monthly outings then no outings, because none of us could face the upside-downness of the pineapple cake in the chiller cabinet. Sage said, 'It's time to forget Joe-Romeo and be true to yourselves,' but our selves were so packed with thermal images of the man from Wisconsin who could speak the language of the universe, there was no room for truth.

Around this time, classes at Karma Yoga started to overrun by ten minutes. Sage had us planking like ironing boards were going out of fashion. We swore silently at her, at the dim fairy lights, at the mean window that looked out onto the lovelessness of concrete and shattered glass. For a while, things were really dire.

Then one day she brought Tibetan sound bowls to class and said she would tweak our vagus nerves and reset our outlook on life. But vibrating bowls would never compete with the Om of Joe-Romeo. She was kidding none of us. Still, we laid ourselves out in shavasana each week like so many spatchcocked chickens under orders to rest, while she bashed her bowls and let base notes and top notes fade towards nothingness before bashing some more. Time is a healer, as they say, but time had little to do with our cure. It was those dying notes, one after another after another, that soon made us dying to be done with dying.

Dying was almost behind us when, one Thursday a year later, Joe-Romeo came back with his dark energy—and new yoga pants covered in silver infinity signs. Joe-Romeo! Our insides fired up like rocket boosters. Sage said, 'Let's celebrate our practice with the sound of a single Om.' And Joe-Romeo would have swallowed us whole—fate, love and second chances—if Sage hadn't picked up her mallet and struck a bowl so hard that it skidded right off its plump silk cushion. Copper circles of sound pulsed across the room, bringing wave after wave of meaning, depriving Joe-Romeo of his dramas, carving up his passions and collapsing his final act. In the crashing silence that followed, the sound of his universe made brilliant sense, and the stars over Tekapo went out.

MEGAN KITCHING

Oxygen

The body without breath is disbelief.
He can no longer lie on this wheeled bed,
in no sense can verbs apply and yet
my brain goes on rocking the prow of his chest,
twitching the sheet over his weeping legs,
revisiting the ward with my words.
Nothing is going in. Oxygen pours
against his mouth like my expectation:
I see him choke awake, grope around tubes
for his glasses on their fishing twine
and tell me to shut that bloody valve to save
wasting air. But the cylinder persists,
indicating numbers in amber,
its deep-sea mass and industrious wheeze
like a third person present, or now a second.
The nurses in their huddle-meeting, when I say
'I don't think he's breathing', gesture me away.
No one can do anything. My distress
beats around the room like a swallow.
The intimate outrage of half a breath
left waiting at the door long past closing,
his Adam's apple rigid as the plastic mask,
my knowing and my refusal to know.
I am in panic at the absolute: how fast
his sun-chafed colour, his ruddiness
of broken vessels estranges yellow-pale.
A chill fades his face, the sparsely freckled brow
remote from my farewell. The huge echo
of too much stopping darkens the oxygen's hiss.
He is already a shade smaller and very final.
I creep up and down so as not to disturb him.

JOSIAH MORGAN

Thirteen Beautiful Things

Your two arms creating a radial disc.
Bookshelves conjoining with sunlight's kiss.
        The wind the weeds conquer.

        Licorice tea that you offer.
Four legs on a chair that cast parallel shadows
And the marks fabricated on your Post-it notes.

        The Farrar, Straus and Giroux anthology.
An absence of touch recorded on me.
        Musical waves as they hit the ground.

        Aniseed flavour, clarinet sound,
A jacket that hangs with no shoulder's shape.
A walk in the day as it's getting too late.

KIM COPE TAIT

Lesbians at a Mormon Dance Party

Three hours after I announce
that I don't know if we exist
beyond the work we do together,
we are at a Mormon
dance party together.
It is a 90s-themed farewell to Ella,
who clearly wishes it was her
you had brought to this party,
but that wouldn't make any sense
of course. I am dressed
like a boy band member,
but you look cool, as ever:
Snoop Dogg vibes and your
signature smirk.
Ella is not dressed up at all.

We float near each other, not
touching. We eat pistachios or
chat about home-school drama—
it's a thing, it turns out.
I have feared this moment
since the invitation went out
on Facebook, and now I attend
only because you have told me that
you don't care whether these people,
almost all of them from your church,
approve of me or not. You say that
there will be no one here you care for
more than you do for me, and
these are the only words

that could have dragged me here tonight.
We both know this.

Everyone is unapologetically sober
but grooving nonetheless—to Warren G,
Salt-N-Pepa, Missy Elliott. There is a
quiet beneath the music but the vibe is
happy. Everyone is unselfconscious,
like only habitually sober people can be.
Something beautiful in it, really—
their children meandering among the
be-bopping adults. The darkness and
flashing of the hand-turned disco ball—
purchased from an op shop—don't bely
the safety of this space,
even for two-year-old Frida.
She goes from person to person
offering caramel corn from her well-licked
baby fingers, and we can't help but eat it.

We make our way
toward each other. The way we hold hands
on the couch when we finally sit
is probably more than anyone bargained for—
it is hard to tell how they feel
about your female partner.
At least I am not
wearing the bucket hat any more.
Ella cries and cries and says
it's about the farewell,
how she's leaving Dunedin
and won't be back any time soon,
but I can see how she loves you.

Later, while your fingers are
tangled in mine, seven-year-old Jessie

climbs onto our combined laps
to be near and inside of this love.
Then she is spirited away
by another child with an idea,
a plan we cannot hear
above TLC singing about waterfalls.
You drape a leg over mine,
don't shy away from loving me here,
though you still have so many questions.
Thank you is a quiet thought that
doesn't reach my lips.

The evening ends when the bishop can't
find his phone and we have to
turn the lights up and the music down.
Only at a Mormon dance party,
I think, and a smile lifts the edges of my lips.
Tonight as we pull up in your driveway,
laughing about the awkwardness
and the sweetness of it all,
gratitude curls itself around my ears
and you invite me to your bed.
We are too tired even to kiss,
and with 90s Snoop Dogg
still ringing in our ears
we fall into the deep sleep
of solace. It is ours,
if only for tonight.
Ella sleeps alone.
I would not trade her happiness
for mine, I know.
I am no saint.
I am the one
who wakes with
your hand
on my ribs.

KIRBY WRIGHT

King Kamehameha

My teats, once supple,
Droop like dying roses

In a crystal vase.
What have I paid for living?

Mouth the nipples
Of mortality

And return me
To teenage years.

Strange how bone
Remains white

After a half-life
Of dark blood rushing

Through skeleton.
I see Hawaiian flesh

Impaled on a rotating pole
Crowned by a foreign flag.

What lies beyond suffering?
Play 'The Star-Spangled Banner'

Backwards and hear
Kamehameha's whimper.

BRETON DUKES

In the Company of Bullies

Dunedin, 1991

Kemp and Pratt came past. Monk, South, then Digger, Digger and his handbag. You selected a runty third-former, loosened that kid's tie, the top few buttons of his shirt, and then, palm out, you jammed your arm down his shirt front, into his undies, out the leg of his shorts, back up to grip the fat end of his tie. Then you carried him off like a handbag.

This one had a tight red face—because of the pain and because you needed to grip on tight to avoid their clothes ripping. Sometimes their scrotum got torn and blood went down the sides of their legs. Sometimes you could get past a teacher with a handbag. Mostly, like now, it was nothing extraordinary. Like, you could have one on your arm and be doing something else altogether. Eating a pie, say, in the canteen, pastry flakes snowing onto the turd's face.

And Digger was in a hostel. So really, this was nothing compared to what he did there. And what he did there was nothing compared to the fact that the manager of the hostel sometimes watched third- and fourth-formers in the shower. And, well, what happened when the lights went out up there probably made the hostel manager's ogling look like candyfloss.

Lunchtime it was. Seventh-form common room. Which meant clubrooms of the Foul Bahesions. Kemp came back by himself and watched Marco spread the four pieces of Molenberg on the chopping board with margarine. Already he'd sliced tasty cheese and opened the can of baked beans. Under the Zip the toastie pie machine was plugged in.

'Red light,' went Kemp.

If anyone else in seventh form had done to their eyebrows what Kemp had done to his they'd be dead.

'Want one?' went Marco.

Kemp nodded. Marco laid the bottom slices, spooned on the beans, added white pepper from the shaker and then carefully set down the cheese and the top layer of bread—making little beds for the beans—then he brought down the lid carefully and latched it in place. Over at the sink he washed his hands and began drying them with a tea-towel.

'You fag,' said Kemp.

Drily, Marco went, 'Thanks.'

They stood there, close together. Marco watched Kemp watch steam come up from the machine. Watched sauce dribble from between crusts that jutted clear. Watched that sauce run, then stop and sizzle when it contacted a hot piece of the machine. Like this, Kemp wasn't that scary. Those two lions down at the Otago Museum in their glass case. Escaped somewhere near Lawrence—terrorising the locals—now what they looked like was little suitcases with legs.

Teachers, especially the younger males, liked to come through occasionally, and late this Thursday lunchtime it was Mr Cheese. He was only a few years older than they all were. He played blindside for Pirates Seniors and most days wore their black, crested club jersey. Today he also wore silver dress trousers and boat shoes and his fringe caught in the air generated by his long stride.

'Cheese,' went some of the boys.

'Pirates?' went Egg, then he coughed, saying *Fag* within the cough, then in a friendlier way, because secretly they were all impressed with Cheese, he said, 'Why not play for Kaikorai?'

He was with a group in the window seat that looked over the library. Nichol had a tennis ball and was hurling it hard across the room, kicking it up and back off the island thing that divided the main part of the room from the kitchenette, and catching it. Now Cheese held out his hand for the ball and Nichol, who played first XI, rifled it in, but instead of a return throw, Cheese kept walking, out through the doors, onto the walkway that was two storeys up, that connected the common room to the science rooms where Marco would go after lunch.

'Fucker,' went Nichol, and just as he did, Cheese stepped back in, cocked his arm and fired the ball across the room, catching Egg clean on the side of the head, causing the ball to zing off at an angle where Knife Menzies, also cricket, dived as if in the gully and took a scorcher, and here now, as the toastie machine light flicked from red to green, the common room detonated into whoops, yowls and, 'Cheese, Cheese, Cheese!' and three first XV guys formed up and stampeded Egg, rucking his back and legs and head with their nomads.

Marco, meanwhile, had two plates ready and with the tip of his forefinger he forced each sandwich loose from where spilled sauce had caramelised, binding the bread to the machine, and once they were plated he went to the quieter side of the room where Kemp was sitting on one of the chairs around the large red table.

'Sir,' went Marco, setting the food down like this was some fancy restaurant. Immediately he was self-conscious but Kemp didn't say anything, just picked his sandwich up and started nibbling the crusts, avoiding the sauce that at this early stage in the eating would burn the shit out of any soft parts of your mouth it made contact with.

'Dad's in hospital,' Marco wanted to say. 'Mum's out of her head,' he wanted to say. But he stayed quiet.

'After this?' went Kemp.

'Physics.'

Kemp grunted. He blew out, cooling the sandwich, and when he took a shallow quick bite, cheese made a swing-bridge from his mouth to the sandwich.

'Stats?' went Marco.

Really, Marco didn't need to ask. Everyone knew Kemp's timetable. It was basic personal safety. Those lions—one being free in town would be bad. And you could carry a gun when you went out of your house. A knife, a bow and arrow. You could make sure to be inside after sundown. But even better than those precautions, *know where the beast is at all times.*

Kemp, in response to Marco's question, made a sad noise into the sandwich he then destroyed with a huge bite. Right into the middle, causing beans to tumble from the side and plop onto his plate and the table. Looking at the mess he'd made, he chewed and then took another bite. In imitation, Marco took big bites of his own. Hot sweet beans, the full flavour of nearly liquid cheese, the soft inside of the bread versus the crunchy outside, the penetrating nasal heat of white pepper.

They ate on, adjusting their hands on the crusts. Looking into the red interior of the things, wiping their mouths, chewing, swallowing, shifting that food from their hands to their mouths, down into their young stomachs.

'I'd root Sheila Sim,' went Marco.

Kemp looked, but didn't say anything.

'Would you?' went Marco.

Kemp sat back a little and looked around the room. In his hand the sandwich was now no more than a length of brown crust. Marco thought of those plastic rectangular lengths used in maths at primary. There were different colours and they had hard edges and each length represented ten or five or one or two and you were to sort of shift them around making different equations.

Primary school—that was something he would have liked to ask Kemp about. He'd had a crush on Glenda Forgie, on Vicky, but who'd been Kemp's crushes? His favourite teachers? What were the popular games at lunchtime? That sort of stuff.

'Killed a dog once,' he would have liked to say. 'Had no choice—this creepy old man was after me.'

Instead, what came out was, 'Tit fuck her, fuck her back hole.'

Kemp's face was neutral. Might be he'd nodded a little when Marco mentioned Sim's arsehole, might just have been his jaw was still working on the toast. Quiet came down between them. Behind, on the other side of the school, was Arthur Street Primary. Kids outside playing their lunch games.

There were the things Marco wanted to say, and there were the things he said, the things he did. Finishing the last section of beans, he threw the crust across the room. It bounced on the carpet and came to a stop near to where what had happened with Egg and Cheese was now evolving into a full scrum. Eight on eight. Taylor there like a ref, Bill Knugg ready to feed ball.

Off to the side, Egg was rubbing the side of his head.

'Looks like he might cry,' went Marco.

The bell rang. Long and loud. Kemp stood. Sensing this, the six boys who made up the two front rows of three looked in Kemp's direction, waiting to see if what they were doing would have any impact. Maybe Kemp would jump onto the roof of one scrum and start coaching, might be he'd pull down the number 8's trousers and boxers and wrench his cock back between his legs, sticking it with spit back into the boy's crack, might be he'd punch someone.

But Kemp veered off to the door to the stairs, shouldering his bag, shouldering his way into the stairwell, taking everything out of the room with him, so the scrum disassembled, the locks standing and flattening their hair, the flankers rising off their knees, saying *Fag* to their opposite, *Fucking fag* while they searched out their school bags, bags their mums had got them at Arthur Barnett's back in fifth form, filled with lunch bags, with named 1B5 books, with Jumbo Sketch Pads, with gridded maths books, with tubular pencil cases emblazoned with the words Pencil Case where boys had written the names of bands or changed Pencil to Penis, where inside the case were HB pencils, BIC pens, rubbers, protractors, compasses, corrugated pencil shavings, coins for bus fares, folded scraps of paper featuring badly drawn cunts, featuring lists of the best All Black back lines ever, featuring hearts with arrows going through, featuring stick figure sex drawings detailing sodomy, oral sex, doggy style.

★

Marco took out his physics book and pencil case. He got a black pen and clicked it a few times, closely watching the mechanism. With the jagged edge of a can's lid you could slice your wrists up. He thought about where exactly he could sit while he bled out, but he didn't think about it for long. Sheila Sim he thought about. Glenda. Kemp. That morning Mum had said she needed him to make less noise around the house.

'What do you mean?'

'Just be bloody quieter.'

'But when, like—'

'Walking, closing doors, putting the lid back on the peanut butter. *Everything.*' She'd put her hand up by his face and for a moment he'd thought she might touch his cheek or his neck but what she'd done was make a motion with her thumb and forefinger like her fingers were working a little knob. 'Turn the volume down. You think I want to be reminded of all this all the time?' She gestured around at the kitchen. Marco didn't really understand.

'What's going to happen with Dad?'

'Oh, *that man*. Go on—away, go. Go, goddamnit. Take yourself and all your noise out the front door.'

Other boys entered the classroom. Then Mr Banks. He was finishing an apple and he nodded when he saw Marco. Then he went to his desk in the corner of the room, dropped the core in the grey metal rubbish bin and wiped his hands on a handkerchief he carefully drew from the pocket of his sports jacket. He went to the whiteboard, where he'd fixed an array of markers with Blu-Tack—ammo on an ammo belt was how they looked—to the lower right side of the board, and after considering for a moment he selected the blue pen and walked to the other end of the whiteboard, removing the lid and fitting it into the base of itself. Then, his free hand on his hip, he stretched up and began writing.

Banks was Marco's Second XV coach. He was an old boy, had played First XV a decade back, and later on, out on Littlebourne, he'd be working closely with Marco and the other backs, formulating cunning new moves for that Saturday's big game against the John McGlashan First XV. On a bus one time coming back from a game against Tokomairiro High, Banks had told Marco he wasn't that far off the First XV—that if it wasn't for all the FOB Coconuts the school had brought down from Auckland he'd definitely have been in the firsts and that either way after school he'd have a good career in club rugby.

As a teacher Banks was known as a mean fucker. When Marco was a turd, the rumours were that Banks and Ms B, the drama teacher, were together, but that was years ago, and really, other than his breath, the weird way he wore his hair, and how all you did in his class was copy shit off the whiteboard, hardly anyone said anything about Banks these days.

After Tuesday's practice they'd all been in a big circle out near halfway and Banks said a few things about tactics and preparation and then gave the floor to Magus, head of the hostel, hooker and captain.

'Might as well kill ourselves if we fuck this up,' went Magus. 'Hands up who wants to lose to a pack of private-school faggots?'

Remembering that, looking at Banks's back, Marco, like he was still in that circle, like he actually had some balls, raised his arm up above his head before letting it collapse onto the desk. Then Kelvin Sempler came in. Marco hadn't thought about him all day but just the sight of his out-sized grey school bag—like a fucking space shuttle strapped to his back—did something to Marco's bowels. And as Sempler took that bag off, saying nothing but making brief eye contact with Marco, basically knowing exactly what was coming, Marco stood a little, and just as that very specific rectal pressure built he reached down the back of his own undies, got his hand into position and, as his anus relaxed he caught the fart, feeling its wind against his palm. Standing fully, he took Sempler by the back of his head and got that fart hand right in under Sempler's nose. Sempler, who bucked back and went to the side, only fell still when Marco let go of his head and punched him three times on the shoulder, saying, 'You love it, Kelvin, what? You love it.'

Boys around them laughed. At the board, Banks had stopped writing but remained facing the board, and only now, as Marco sat back down, as Sempler rubbed his face and arm and also sat, reaching into that stupid fucking school bag, did the teacher turn, and was that a thin smile he gave Marco? Either way, people calmed real fast, not just because of Banks and his reputation, but because nothing about this was extraordinary. Marco had been catching farts for Sempler since halfway through term one, since the day Sempler turned up wearing black shoes that were unlike anything anyone else wore—pocked in neat swirls, with an actual heel, made with different pieces of leather. And though Sempler hadn't worn those shoes again, the farting thing was just a bit of a fun, a bit of sport, a bit of a tradition, and wasn't the rector and pretty much every fucker around this place always going on about traditions and how important they were?

JESSICA LE BAS

Coming to the End of the Red Apple

When someone asks what it was like—
            And again, you are taking that first crunchy bite,
the sweet juice rolling from your lips, your chin wet,
its flesh cold against the inside of your mouth

            And that second bite, more sumptuous
even, because now your expectations are raised
You reach up, wipe the juice from your face
to do it all over again—that effervescent fizz
            and you almost sneezing
And so it goes, the eating of the apple

Its shiny red side first, turned then to the
dull part, where once it faced away from the sun

You bite down hard, till you have gone full circle
and only the core is left, and you nibble slowly,
with the very edge of your front teeth. Savour
those last little pieces of pulp

Then you bite, unintended of course, into a pip,
which leads you to retract, to feel cheated somehow
O how you suddenly ache to go back
            to that first crisp mouthful

All that is left in your hand is a gnarly stalk
and an edge of withered skin. Not even
the skeleton of your former self. Not even.

JOANNA PASCOE

Sisyphus at Kā Roimata o Hine Hukatere Glacier

Heading out to sea
glacial water rollicks grey blue
over stones rubbed smooth,
endophytes grow in the ancient forest: harakeke on rata.

Glacial water rollicks grey blue.
Sisyphus rolls the boulder past a moa,
endophytes grow in the ancient forest: harakeke on rata.
He stops to wrap his feet in soft moss.

Sisyphus rolls the boulder past a moa,
a sandfly nibbles on his flesh, between finger and thumb.
He stops to wrap his feet in soft moss.
Pushing up the moraine, he pauses to wipe sweat from his brow.

A sandfly nibbles on his flesh, between finger and thumb.
Ice underfoot, he's glad of the green warmth.
Pushing up the moraine, he pauses to wipe sweat from his brow.
He finds a path left by long-horned tahr and creeps to the precipice.

Ice underfoot, he's glad of the green warmth.
Hovering—him and his stone,
he finds a path left by long-horned tahr and creeps to the precipice.
It's beautiful up here.

Hovering—him and his stone
at the apex, the oxygen is thin.
It's beautiful up here.
He starts to laugh.

At the apex, the oxygen is thin.
Teetering—off balance,
he starts to laugh,
the boulder begins its descent.

Teetering—off balance,
gathering speed, it races down a shingle scree,
the boulder begins its descent,
gracefully.

Gathering speed, it races down a shingle scree.
Sisyphus follows, like a parallel skier,
gracefully,
bobbing up and down

over stones rubbed smooth,
heading out to sea.

BRENT KININMONT

That Stage

A lung check, an aunt recalls,
was part of the physical.

Around the plastic tube
her smoker husband wrapped

his lips. Picture candles,
the doctor told him, and blow.

The slider darted off,
stopped too abruptly.

Beside him she pictured
a packed town hall.

He'd once driven her down from Waitaki
for Louis Armstrong.

More of a crooner by that stage
than a trumpeter.

JACKSON C. PAYNE

Company Rule

I turn crank. I do not ask what crank does. Asking what crank does adds one day of crank turning to Predetermined Retirement Date. Additional days of crank turning after Predetermined Retirement Date: 757. This is because father died two years out from retirement. Company Rule number 88: *The Children of the Parents who cannot fulfil their Duties to The Company will take on those Duties until paid in Full*. With no further extensions I will retire at age seventy-seven.

So. I turn crank.

Just like my father turned crank and his father turned crank but no one talks about the father before his because that was too many crank turns ago.

Beside me, Clung. Clung is pulley winder. We are not supposed to talk but sometimes when Supervisor is at the other end of Work Quadrant, we converse. Clung comes from a long line of pulley winders. His father's father's father etc etc etc.

Today, as I turn crank and Clung winds pulley, Clung asks, *Why do you turn crank?*

Easy, I say. *Same reason you wind pulley.*

Sometimes Clung is a joker and I think he is joking but he is not.

Clung says, *But why do we do this every day?*

I say, *To repay our Debt to Colossal Glob. You know this.*

Clung says, *Why do we have Debt to Colossal Glob?*

I say, *Everyone has Debt to Colossal Glob.*

Clung says, *I know The Company says we have Debt to Colossal Glob but I do not know why.*

I say, *Yes, you do. So we can go to The Next Place.*

Clung says, *But how do we know The Next Place exists? And how do we know Colossal Glob is real?*

I am stunned. Company Rule number 2: *Do not question The Company's link to Colossal Glob. Doing so will lead to Eternity of Damnation.*

Supervisor returns to our sector of Work Quadrant so I cannot express my stunnedness.

So. I turn crank.

Clung winds pulley.

★

Tonight in Designated Rest Area (DRA) I rehydrate my daily allocation of Vitamin Concentrate. Packaging states flavour: Beef Steak. I have never tried Beef Steak but if it is like Vitamin Concentrate then I do not wish to try Beef Steak. Vitamin Concentrate makes inside of lips stick to gums. But after sixteen hours of Requisite Work Activity, Vitamin Concentrate is not so bad.

While trying to unstick gums from teeth I think about Clung. I also think about Company Rule number 54: *All Devotees must report any known Digressions to Supervisor or risk adding one year (365 days) of Work Activity to Predetermined Retirement Date.* I think: What if, by not reporting Clung, I add 365 days to my Predetermined Retirement Date? I will then be seventy-eight. And then I think: Damn you, Clung. And then I think: But Clung is Friend. Clung is Only Friend.

I look at Father's Sleeping Compartment in DRA: just as he left it. Grey sheet pulled tight around foam mattress. Solitary decoration on wall: Piece of paper found on floor of Work Quadrant that reads 'Marlboro'. He did not learn what this 'Marlboro' was before death. Company Rule number 300: *Devotees must not ask Questions about anything other than Work.*

And then I think: What would Father do about Clung?

*

I arrive at Work Quadrant before commencement of Work to report Clung to Supervisor but Clung is already conversing with Supervisor. Clung and Supervisor look as though they are conversing about me.

I go to Work Station.

So. I turn crank.

Clung returns to Work Station. He winds pulley.

After 3.5 hours of Requisite Work Activity, Supervisor makes his way to other end of Work Quadrant.

Clung says, *You were at Work Quadrant early today. I have never known you to arrive at Work Quadrant so early.*

I say, *I could not sleep.*

Clung says, *Why could you not sleep?*

I say, *Because I was thinking of you breaking Company Rules.*

Clung says, *Why do we follow Company Rules?*

I say, *You know why we follow Company Rules. To not add additional years to Predetermined Retirement Date.*

Clung says, *But why is it important to get to Predetermined Retirement Date?*

I say, *So we can Retire.*

Clung says, *Who do you know who has Retired?*

I say, *We all know those who have retired. Like Blorn, from Maintenance. We all received 2.5 Free Work Minutes to wave him goodbye during the last Financial Quarter.*

Clung says, *Yes, but who do you know from this Work Quadrant to have Retired?*

I cannot think of anyone from this Work Quadrant who has Retired. I try. But I cannot.

So. I turn crank.

Clung winds pulley.

★

When I arrive at DRA my Spectrovisual Entertainment Device is sitting on desk. For one hour this evening we can have Allocated Relaxation experiences beyond Work Quadrant and DRA. Excuse me, not can, must. Company Rule number 253: *All Devotees are to Engage Positively in any Activity deemed by The Company to be of benefit to the Devotee. Failure to do so will lead to extension of Predetermined Retirement Date by one week (seven days) per Breach.*

The Spectrovisual Entertainment Device allows us to see and feel many things from before the Great Intervention of Colossal Glob. For example, we can partake in different types of Gainful Employment. I am partial to setting: Household Chores. But my favourite: Shopping at Supermarket. So much choice!

I rehydrate Vitamin Concentrate. Tonight's flavour: Spaghetti Bolognese. I do not know what Spaghetti Bolognese tastes like but if it tastes anything like Vitamin Concentrate then I do not wish to try Spaghetti Bolognese.

After Vitamin Concentrate I pick up the Spectrovisual Entertainment Device. A note falls out. It reads: 'Turn to setting "Abaddon".—Clung'

I look around DRA as if to find Clung. I do not find Clung. I also do not see how he entered DRA. I also do not know what 'Abaddon' is.

I think: Why does Clung do this? I think: Clung has broken many more Company Rules by entering DRA. I think: If I do not Report Clung, I will prolong my Predetermined Retirement Date. And I think: Why does Clung want me to see 'Abaddon'?

I will not let Clung ruin my one hour of Allocated Relaxation.

So. I put on the Spectrovisual Entertainment Device. I switch it to: Shopping at Supermarket.

Near the baked goods I smell fresh bread. It must be what The Next Place smells like. I stand there breathing it in. I walk the aisles of fresh fruit and vegetables. The colours! At Work Sector: Grey. At DRA: Mostly grey, some black. But the fruit and vegetables: All colours imaginable. I want to take a bite of each fruit, each vegetable. But one thing Spectrovisual Entertainment Device does not allow for: Taste.

I make my way to: Meat. My skin tingles from the refrigerator. I look at the meats. Chicken. Pork. Beef. Tenderloin. T-bone. Ribeye. What was it to have food that does not make lips stick to gums? I touch the cool packaging and wonder: How does meat become meat? I know it was animals but I do not know what happens in between.

I then go to aisle: Breakfast Cereal. At the end of Breakfast Cereal: Clung. I think: How is Clung in my Spectrovisual Projection? This has never happened. I bypass my favourite breakfast foods and confront Clung. Clung does not say anything when I ask: *Why are you in my Spectrovisual Projection?* Clung looks like Clung but also not like Clung. Clung flickers like he will disappear. Clung's mouth moves but I cannot hear him. I move my ear close to this mouth. Still nothing. I go closer still and then he is screaming. It is so loud I think I will lose consciousness from the pain. I rip the Spectrovisual Entertainment Device from my head.

On table in front of me in DRA: Clung's note.

I wait for pain in ears to stop. I put Spectrovisual Entertainment Device back on. I switch it to setting: Abaddon.

Hot needles stabbing at my spine. It feels as if someone's hands are closing around my neck. I cannot breathe. I think: This is how I die. And then I think: Damn you, Clung. And then I lose consciousness.

*

I wake up on the floor of DRA. Spectrovisual Entertainment Device nowhere to be seen. It is many hours after commencement of Work. Company Rule number 192: *All Devotees to Practise Punctuality in preparation for meeting with Colossal Glob. Failure to Practise Punctuality will lead to extension of Predetermined Retirement Date by one week (seven days) for every hour of Requisite Work Activity missed.*

I hurry to Work Quadrant.

At Work Quadrant Clung winds pulley.

I try to catch Clung's eye but he does not look up.

Supervisor arrives.

Supervisor says, That is twenty-eight days' extension to Predetermined Retirement Date. Do you accept? If so, sign here.

He hands me clipboard on which is Extension Notice.

I say, But I am only three hours late.

Supervisor holds up Personal Metric Odometer, which shows three seconds into the fourth hour of lateness.

I sign Extension Notice.

So. I turn crank.

Supervisor spends many more hours than usual in this sector of Work Quadrant. Supervisor leaves just minutes before end of Work Activity. When he does, I say to Clung, Why are you doing this to me?

Clung says, as if unaware, Doing what?

I say, Breaking Company Rules. Tampering with my Spectrovisual Entertainment Device.

Clung says, But I did not tamper with your Spectrovisual Entertainment Device.

I say, But what about the note?

Clung says, What note?

And then it is the end of Work Activity so we can no longer converse. Company Rule number 83: *Devotees must not converse with other Devotees coming to or going from Work Quadrant.*

So. I return to DRA and rehydrate Vitamin Concentrate. Tonight's flavour: Chicken Parmigiana. It tastes like Beef Steak and Spaghetti Bolognese. Lips stick to gums more vigorously than usual.

★

I arrive at Work Quadrant very early. So early I know Clung will not be there. So early Work Quadrant doors remain locked.

Supervisor arrives to unlock Work Quadrant.

Supervisor says I cannot start early to make up missed hours. Extension Notice has been signed.

I say, I am aware of Company Rule number 27. I am here to talk to you about Clung.

Supervisor says, Who is Clung?

I say, Clung. The pulley winder stationed next to me in Work Quadrant.

Supervisor says, Oh, you mean Varden.

I say, Varden?

Supervisor says, Yes, Varden. The wheel spinner stationed next to you in Work Quadrant.

I say, Oh yes, Varden.

I do not know a Varden.

Supervisor says, And what is it you wish to tell me about Varden?

I say, Varden is an excellent wheel spinner. I have never seen anyone spin wheels with such enthusiasm.

Supervisor says, Is that all?

I nod my head and attend Work Station.

Several minutes later a man I have never seen before arrives at Work Station next to mine. The Work Station where Clung used to wind pulley. The man waits for commencement of Work and starts to spin wheel.

When Supervisor makes his way to the other end of Work Quadrant I converse with the wheel spinner.

I say, *What is your name?*

He says, *You are such a joker, Clung!*

I say, *Clung? My name is not Clung.*

He says, laughing, *All right then, today I am Clung and you are Varden. You are such a joker.*

After a time he stops laughing.

So. I turn crank.

Varden spins wheel.

And then I say, *Why do you spin wheel?*

Varden says, *Same reason you turn crank.*

I say, *But why do we do this every day?*

Varden says, *To repay our Debt to Colossal Glob.*

I say, *Why do we have Debt to Colossal Glob?*

Varden says, *Everyone has Debt to Colossal Glob.*

I say, *I know The Company says we have Debt to Colossal Glob but I do not know why.*

He says, *Yes you do. So we can go to The Next Place.*

I say, *But how do we know The Next Place exists?*

Varden looks at me strangely, opens his mouth as if to say something, but Supervisor returns to our sector of Work Quadrant.

So. Varden spins wheel.

I turn crank.

*

At DRA I do not feel like rehydrating Vitamin Concentrate. I think: Where is Clung? And then I think: Who is Varden? And then I think: Why does Varden think that I am Clung? And then I think: Company Rule number 352: *Devotees to The Company must consume all Provisions allocated to them or risk extension to Predetermined Retirement Date.*

So. I rehydrate Vitamin Concentrate.

I do not bother checking flavour but I note that, as usual, lips stick to gums.

I take piece of paper with 'Marlboro' on it from wall of father's Sleeping Compartment. I study 'Marlboro'. I wonder what it could mean. Is Marlboro connected to Colossal Glob? The Company's *Official Testimony of Colossal Glob* does not mention this Marlboro. I think: How did 'Marlboro' paper get into Work Quadrant? And then I think: Why do I care? Before Clung said anything about non-existence of Colossal Glob, I was happy turning crank. Now when I turn crank, I think: Why do I turn crank?

I turn 'Marlboro' paper over. On the back I find a note. It reads: 'Dear Varden. If you are reading this then I have left Work Quadrant. Maybe I have gone to The Next Place. Maybe even another place. Remember: Work hard and always spin wheel with dedication. Love, Father.'

★

At Work Quadrant I deliver 'Marlboro' paper with note to Supervisor.

I say, *Supervisor, somehow this note for Varden made its way into my DRA.*

Supervisor looks at me. Squints. Tilts his head. Says nothing.

I say, *Can you please give this to Varden?*

Supervisor says, *But you are Varden.*

I say, *No, I am Clung.*

Supervisor says, *Clung? Who is Clung? Please stop wasting my time, Varden. Return to your Work Station and commence Requisite Work Activity.*

I return to Work Station but I do not find crank. Instead, I find wheel.

So. I spin wheel.

Next to me is Varden. Or who I think is Varden.

Varden pumps lever.

When Supervisor leaves our sector of Work Quadrant I ask Varden, *What is your name?*

He says, *You are such a joker, Varden.*

I say, *But you are Varden.*

He laughs and says, *Okay, today I am Varden and you can be Dweef.*

I say, *Dweef?*

Dweef says, *I am Varden. Today, you are Dweef.*

★

After Requisite Work Activity I follow Varden. I mean, I follow Dweef. At DRA Dweef goes inside. I knock at door but there is no answer. I knock several times: Nothing. So. I go inside. I call out Varden's name and then I remember that he is Dweef. I call out to Dweef. Again there is no answer.

Dweef's DRA is the same as my DRA. There is even father's Sleeping Compartment. On the wall: Piece of paper with 'Marlboro' on it. I untack

'Marlboro' from wall and turn it over. On the back a note reads: 'Dear Dweef. If you are reading this then I have I left Work Quadrant. Maybe I have gone to The Next Place. Maybe even to another place. Remember: Always ask, *Why? Why am I here? Why do I pump lever? Why must I repay my Debt to Colossal Glob?* These questions will guide you. Love, Father.'

I leave note on table and leave Dweef's DRA. I walk the corridors but cannot find my own DRA. It is as though I have forgotten its location. I walk and search. I pass several Supervisors who check their Personal Metric Odometers.

I have three minutes to find DRA. Company Rule number 203: *All Devotees of The Company must domicile in their Designated Rest Areas from 2100 hours until 0500 hours.*

I start to run. I run and I find the corridors somehow become more familiar. Out of breath, I find the door to my DRA. I go inside. On the table is the piece of paper with 'Marlboro' on it. I turn it over. It reads: 'Dear Dweef...'

★

I do not go to Work Quadrant for Requisite Work Activity. I stay in DRA, prostrate in Sleeping Compartment. I look at grey ceiling. I think of Clung. Or was it Varden? And then I think of Dweef. What did Dweef say? *Today, you are Dweef.* But that was yesterday. Today is today. Today, am I still Dweef? I am in Dweef's DRA. But who is Dweef?

And then I think of Blorn. I think of him retiring at seventy-five, on Predetermined Retirement Date, no extensions. I think of Blorn waving, smiling, walking through door to The Next Place.

Time passes slowly when not participating in Requisite Work Activity. Turning crank does not make time go fast, but faster than staying in DRA. Or do I spin wheel? Or pump lever? I cannot tell. I calculate the extension to Predetermined Retirement Date after full day of no Requisite Work Activity. A third of a year of crank turns/wheel spins/lever pumps.

There is a knock at the door.

Outside there is no one. On the ground is a Spectrovisual Entertainment Device. I pick it up and a note falls out. It reads: 'Turn to setting "Standard Work Day".—Dweef.'

So. I put on Spectrovisual Entertainment Device. I switch it to setting: Standard Work Day.

I am at Work Quadrant.

So. I turn crank.

Beside me: Clung. Clung winds pulley. Clung asks, *Why do you turn crank?*

RACHEL O'NEILL

The Lantern of Fear Sausage Sizzle

The kid on the grill is good. Technically a bit quotational. I suspect the use of Pepper's Ghost. Yeah, he's definitely off stage, brightly lit and using a mirror projection. Still, each time his illusion flips a sausage my mouth waters. Given the Machiavellian length of the queue, he prefers to warm punters up by way of enforced 'fasting' rather than drugs or the fatigue of a night sizzle, platformed in total and murderous darkness. Note the dog sniffing the Radcliffean tongs. Could it be an expansion of Benjamin on Marx where the phantasmagorical supremacy of the commodity is stripped of hierarchy not by means of thunder, aromatic smoke or a glass harmonica but caramelised onion? 'What would you like on it …?' The shade of the eleven-year-old charlatan asks with the weariness of a despotic Archduke facing expulsion from Prussia. Squirting red sauce on the bread he deftly removes his head from his neck and places it by the serviettes before putting it back on again. But this is nothing compared to what he pulls off outside the Wedding Expo with some skeletal doves, a ghost groom and a palace with a broken wheel, leading to police intervention and a heart attack of bridesmaids described by one journalist as 'terribly mathematically exact'.

SHELLEY BURNE-FIELD

The Fat Girl

A tribute to OM

When the fat girl arrived, she did not wind like a river through the town. She had a low centre of gravity and popped up smiling on street corners, no thigh gap in sight. She sat on armless chairs at the one café in town, her bum hanging over edges. Her favourite order was guacamole and blue corn chips, and she settled in as though she'd always been etched into the stone walls of the town, one day showing herself like a storm at night, though no one knew her name.

The leader of the local Butterfly Book Group, Annette Hudson, shut down any gossip and squashed all talk of stereotype. Despite the fat girl's sensual lips, she carried a mysterious aura, Annette said, not exotic exactly, but with an olive complexion reminiscent of the Mediterranean. Plus, there must be an interesting backstory contained in the follicles of her mid-length, electric-blue hair. Perhaps she was a teacher?

The fat girl volunteered a lot. One autumnal Saturday, at the bowling club, an octogenarian nana in a white smock twittered on ex-ballet toes and asked the fat girl—who was mucking in already—to dish out saucers of cheese with two crackers and to serve cups of teapot tea. After the five o'clock swill she mopped up shandies spilt on tables and urine splashed on skirting boards. Then the fat girl drove the club courtesy van and stopped to buy milk and bread so the bowlers didn't go home empty handed. They considered the fat girl in the same manner as one of the collectible teaspoons used to stir their tea—useful and nicely curved.

People claimed to live next door to her. Once, a toddler and his mother met the fat girl at a shared food exchange table down the street. The boy pointed at her legs and shouted excitedly, all the while giggling. Nobody knew what he was saying until his mother blushed and whispered behind her hand that he was calling out, 'Fat! Fat! Fat!'. The fat girl grinned and patted his head.

It was as though the fat girl pleased everyone but mostly herself, which left a certain taste in people's mouths. They couldn't put their finger on it. She blended so well; she was the perfect pastel smudge. When it rained, it didn't stop her standing outside supermarkets selling raffle tickets for the SPCA. When the sun burned, she still crafted coconut cakes and organised the PTA cake stall under a gazebo—even though she had no children to shade.

The fat girl had many fingers in many pies and was the very definition of a savvy charitable soul. She helped feed rough sleepers by bringing them mince on toast. The popular act kept the malodorous beings from begging in front of the pharmacy during busy Friday mornings.

She sang in a charity choir at Christmas in the Park and was smart enough to be seen leaving around 9pm, well before the choir mistress was caught chugging bottles of red wine and pashing the mayor's husband behind the memorial rose bushes.

There was a sweet aura that swirled all around her body, as though her round shoulders were plump enough to shed a tear upon, and her bosom buxom enough to drown out even the fiercest social media blitzkrieg—especially when she wore gingham.

Dogs loved the fat girl. Dr Baird's Labradoodle, Master Farquhar, didn't growl, didn't bite, didn't jump up at her with soiled paws, but sat bowed and let the fat girl scratch behind his ears.

When the fat girl had been in the town for what seemed like a millennium, the chair of the Professional Business Women's group invited her to join, even though the fat girl didn't run a business as such. The Country Women's Institute invited her to their monthly meetings too, as long as she poured the tea in her magical way and brought one of her famous walnut fudge cakes. They oohed and aahed over the fat girl's air of mystery, her possible gypsy heritage (had her swarthy skin tone darkened lately?), and her impeccable work ethic.

Surprisingly, she was found to be a gifted athlete. She aced smallbore and archery competitions by shooting the tightest clusters. The week she joined the track and field club, she beat the mayor's sister in the shotput, out-threw the police commissioner's niece in the discus, and if she had attempted the javelin, there was no doubt the fat girl would have taken that medal from the iwi chair's mokopuna too.

She became woven into the community, while the threads holding her in place were never quite revealed. She remained unreadable: always in the thick of it, but never engaging heart to heart. It began to seem like a chore to truly get to know her at all. Any move towards befriending the fat girl seemed akin to walking through kauri sap: a pointless expenditure of energy.

As a longtime social worker put it, if the fat girl wasn't ready to become vulnerable and wear her heart on her puffed sleeve like the rest of them, then there was little anyone could do. And so the fat girl became part of the furniture, though never exceedingly comfortable or sought after.

She had money. A local real estate agent sold a farm to the fat girl and found her knowledge of the property market deep and full of interesting insights. She knew the history of the area, from chemical hotspots contaminated by tanalised wood mills to old rubbish dump sites beside the river, right back to ancient pā hidden by pine plantations or built over by the ancestors of fifth-generation settlers.

She oozed shrewdness at dinner parties when talk turned to reforming the district plan. Her knowledge of land use showed surprising expertise, to the point that one evening, over a dainty plate of smoked salmon mousse, the fat girl suggested registering wāhi tapu interest in a previously productive piece of land. After a lengthy pause in the conversation she casually threw in that she'd recently discovered twenty-three sleeping pits, a row of palisades and several metres of middens in the corner of a private estate.

Thankfully, the career politician in situ pulled the shocked diners into much safer territory by mentioning that urgent fundraising was required for the new outdoor hockey courts. He then called for the fat girl's excellent strawberry cupcake recipe. The fat girl's lurch into ideological sludge was righted in the space between a plate of fish and a ramekin of smashed meringue, but she had lost a certain lustre.

One day the fat girl turned up at a café wearing a bandage wrapped around her enormous left calf muscle. Her leg had swelled to the size of a pigskin rugby ball and she sat eating a jam donut with her leg sticking out into the aisle. Murray Primmer recalled later at the federation meeting that her eyes seemed pinched and squinty. He also reported that he'd peered over his flat white and seen that her cankles had the shine of pickled pork hocks. She looked puffier than usual.

The following week people noticed her limping along Wakefield Street and coughing into a white handkerchief. She had high colour on her cheeks. She stumbled through piles of autumn leaves and sneezed right beside Nanny Norma's front wheel.

'Gesundheit,' Nanny said to the fat girl, whose face looked like a big old sweating plum. 'You okay, e kare?' But the fat girl coughed again and stumbled past Nanny Norma's mobility scooter.

When citizens began to fall ill with a mysterious flu, it took a nano-second before Kiri Kay, who worked on reception at the local health centre, made the only logical connection: hadn't the fat girl just returned from somewhere foreign? Hadn't she been very sick? Perhaps she'd caught something? Brought it back?

A week later at the café, empty tables and chairs filled the room. The street outside held no echoes. The town felt dampened. Alma Wilkerson had died of the sickness, as had her neighbour, Percy Tawhiti. The school had to be closed, and the bottle store.

When the fat girl once again visited the café, hanky held to her mouth, the owner stepped back as if confronted by a horror. He sent her out the door, then picked up his phone.

'Wtf?' he texted his daughter. 'Patient zero just breathed on me, *again*.'

Her rosy glow had dulled. Even her participation within the justice system had morphed lately into a curse rather than a blessing. She had once counselled victims of crime and made cheese rolls for the constabulary. Behind the wire at the local clink her rehabilitation programmes were the stuff of legend. However, Natalie Pellerman, whose 'Recidivist Resist' programme had never quite met the funding criteria, now had everything to say about it.

'You know her relatives dish out those contracts,' Natalie said with more than a little acid.

The fat girl's halo dropped even further—and became a bullseye on her back. When a plague of locusts exploded through the district, the fat girl was to blame. She'd noticed a pestilent shadow on the moon and evacuated forthwith, but not before leading a whole hedge of rough sleepers to safety. They clambered up the hill while the insects raged through the Roundup Ready crops below. Her kawakawa plantation remained untouched. Not everyone was as fortunate.

'How did that fatty know?'

'She got a special warning. It's not right.'

It didn't take long before the fat girl and her homeless army were reported for looting copper pipe from the bowling club's mower shed. The nerve! Committee members recognised the glint of her greasy blue hair on the security video—though the tape was mysteriously erased before police could take a look. The bowlers were not surprised that the fat girl had taken up with the ferals. She'd always had a shifty look.

'It's those types that gamble their rent money,' the greenkeeper buzzed through his electrolarynx before skipping out to catch the jackpot at the Golden Egg Gaming Lounge.

It was the young mother who chewed the ends of her hair who disputed the talk in the town. 'But she makes such nice fry bread. Is she truly evil?' she asked the owner of Charleenz Hair Salon, just as she was about to get shampooed.

Charlene pulled out her sharp scissors. 'You've only lived here—what?—seventeen years? Not quite a local, eh.'

Kiri Kay, in the middle of a five-hour perm, had just finished telling everybody her cousin from Taihape had *sworn* black and red he'd tattooed the word NOTORIOUS on the fat girl's leg and it had festered up. That explained the bandage. When the young mother sat up from the sink, water dribbling into her ears, she spied the fat girl limping up the steps to the salon.

Every head under a hair dryer turned to watch the moon-faced, enormous thing lurch closer and closer to the glass door. The fat girl reached out but before she could turn the handle, Kiri Kay leapt up and snibbed the lock.

'Yahtzee,' breathed Charlene, welcoming the mother back to the chair for a well-earned head massage.

And so the fat girl's silhouette, once accepted, became a phantom to the people of the town. Her hair now toxic as a poison-dart frog. Her soul as rotten as an offal pit out the back of the farm.

The PTA declined her offers to help with fundraising. They made up the cake-stall shortfall with weekly wine and beer raffles. The choir no longer had space for a contralto, and Master Farquhar was encouraged to squeeze out a turd on her driveway every single morning.

Though she was an invisible entry on an unofficial blacklist, the fat girl continued to appear on the streets with a smile on her jowls that nothing seemed to shake loose. That was until Annette Hudson got a whiff of crack.

It must have been Wednesday evening, said Annette. Out by the old Freemasons building. She remembered clearly because she'd just been to her weekly weigh-in and she'd seen—the Lord help them all, but it was true!—she'd seen with her *own eyes* the fat girl riding pillion on the back of a Big Dog chopper, with her labia pushed up tight against the patched president of the local chapter of Mobs on Hogs.

When somebody mentioned that the fat girl's private parts would hardly have been seen in such a position, Annette's eldest son, Constable Ryan Hudson, related that he'd observed the fat girl out and about one rainy Tuesday and was startled to see that her bits were more moose knuckle than camel toe.

'Her mons pubis seemed, ah, quite prominent,' he mumbled and rubbed the stubble on his chin. 'I'm not sure *she's* even a *she*.'

An audible gasp set things in motion. Constable Ryan—holding his mother's arm—choked up and revealed that the police had uncovered the fat girl's foul plan: to stain the town with enough drugs and depravity that it could never be bleached out, starting with an innocent member of his own family.

According to the constable, the fat girl and two gang molls had lured his father to a hotel that rented rooms by the hour. After 123 minutes Herb had heard a divine voice in his head calling him and managed to escape most of the illicit smoking as well as some of the sodomy. Annette told the Butterfly Book Group that her husband had thought he was going there to sell protein powder.

The community held an extra-extraordinary general meeting.

Acting secretary Natalie Pellerman took the minutes. She adjusted her pink hood, the pointy end having folded in on itself. She breathily explained that she would rather *die* than watch her husband get bummed by a fat girl and two young brown women or men—wasn't that called a foursome? Or so she'd heard. It was the final straw.

The streets were no longer safe. Had they ever been, since the fat girl had sloped into town? She'd groomed them like a gymnast's grubby-fingered coach.

Side-arms were issued. Children gathered strategic piles of rocks in case an opportunistic stoning could be launched. Loofah back scrubbers were soaked in fuel. Somebody tied a noose. The fat girl had shown her devil-dark colours. She'd flooded the town with her true nature. She'd raged like a river through people's properties and dreams. She had to be stopped.

And with that, Master Farquhar tracked the fat girl to the village green at the end of Main Street. He bailed her up in front of the memorial tree, though he whimpered when she scratched behind his ears for the last time.

Annette Hudson fired the first shot. Everyone jumped at the pistol's boom, but her aim was off. Later, Annette would tell everyone she'd tried to target the back of the filthy girl's blue head, but the bullet struck her left butt cheek and made a strange squelching sound. The fat girl just grinned and stared back over her shoulder, as though something cosmic had stretched a curious veil over the town.

The second attack hurtled from a vintage Iver Johnson shotgun. The daughter of the café owner showed off her legs in her Daisy Dukes and misquoted Trump with pride: 'This what you git when you arm the good guys, mutha f*cka.'

The 18-year-old planted her back heel like a pro and fired both barrels. To her dismay, the pellets hit the fat girl's cellulite and blended into the skin as though she were a chameleon.

The third assault came from an SLR 7.62 semi-auto which rallied off nine rounds in the space of a deep breath. Everyone was waiting for a limb to fly off but the bullets disappeared into the fat girl's armpit, emitting a series of soft thuds like raindrops hitting a velvet pillow.

The fourth shot was a rock thrown by one of the children. It completely missed the fat girl and hit Natalie Pellerman smack bang in the temple, killing her stone dead.

The fifth shot was a bolt fired by the mayor's crossbow—straight into the girl's fat mouth. But the fat girl caught the arrow in her teeth, then licked her fat lips and spat it out at the mayor's feet.

The terrified people surged forward in their trucks, EVs and harvesters, bowled the fat girl over then wound a noose around her neck, the rope getting lost in the folds of skin. A tractor appeared, pulling the rope over a branch. Up, up, up she went, her bones stretching, her clothes stripping from her body which was expanding like the universe.

Her skin turned purple black, like an enormous ripe avocado, a strange hanging fruit, and the body creaked and strained. The people below gasped in wonder and affirmation, and their glee held them glued to the spot. As they cranked her up higher, the growth of her gut accelerated and the fat girl reached a critical BMI, fuller and fatter than ever before. Finally, she laughed and plummeted to the ground, grinding like a glacier through the middle of the village green. In her wake, she left a gigantic hole.

As the entire town peered over the edge of the singularity, an old bowler waved her polishing cloth and breathed a sigh of relief, leaning on the immutable chain of people who held hands and scowled into the infinite blackness.

ERIK KENNEDY

DARVO

The most powerful forces in the universe are
the strong nuclear force, the electromagnetic force,
and the need terrible people have to believe
that they are the victims. The sun never sets on
the empire of grievances. The analysts who bomb
apartment buildings say they have their reasons.
It's bullying to doxx dog-kickers, according to
the Society for Kicking Dogs. Tom Fairweather pushed me
off the top of the slide and I broke my arm, alas.
I later learned that it upset him to see my arm
like that. Sorry. Sorry, I'm trying to fix it!
The bone set straight many years ago, but to Tom it will
always be sickening and wonky, wonkening and sicky
and bent out of plumb, an affront to true direction
and a bad memory of an arm, a naughty arm. Even healed,
my arm to Tom is a reminder of a bad time in his life,
the way flowers remind some people of funerals.

MARY MACPHERSON

study

i study the geographic plant collections on this hillside of even-
handed light grey softness discloses angular gazanias puffs
of purple-red cherry black ligularia underscores lebanese cedars
kahlil gibran lived there a mediterranean terrace often built
for the well-off in hills above hot towns launches skies in this town
last night a young man in a soft-pink hoodie a colour i'd like to wear
yelled you miserable cunt down a weed-filled driveway swaying
muttering up the long road i tugged at you to cross a frightened animal
always tugging a thicket of tugging i only forget through plants
countries of their swelling and blossoming my solitary watching
the many forms of their dying & returning on the other side roses
beckoned over black railings, creamy

VANA MANASIADIS

From **Animal Etymologies**

MONSTER

From *men* 'to think' and therefore 'mania' and therefore 'madness', into which maenads, and therefore females who suckle wild animals, who release lines of wine from the earth, who bind civility to 'mon', and so to 'monument' and so to 'demon'; who remember to pay homage; related also to mneme, mnestra 'memory', as in Klytaemnestra who couldn't forget a daughter, who was known also by Klytaemnester, the 'wooer', who remembered her lover by running a bath διοτι η μητριαρχία μέχρι να φτάσει στην τελική σύγκρουση με την πατριαρχία και στην ήττα από αυτή, πέρασε από δύσκολους δρόμους; surviving, truth be told, in the Clytemnestridae and other copepods who, let's be clear, swallow your massive footprints, your carbon tributes, your propensity to daily amnesia, and then en masse sink to the bottom when they're done

TAIL

From *del* 'long', like a serpent's, like Skylla's, Khimera's or Ekhidna's; and so to 'belonging' and so to inhering, for example to habitat, physiology, other symbiotes; related also to 'longing for' your ancestors, parents, their spinal trace; your coccyx or prehensile print; your infants born with vestiges, tissue, muscle, vessels, up to 12cm long (and who can blame them, small caudate things, wanting to swing from tōtara?) Διότι ήταν ένα μόνο ον που είχε τη δύναμη τριών θηρίων, το μπροστινό μέρος ενός λιονταριού, την ουρά ενός δράκου και το τρίτο—το μεσαίο—κεφάλι ενός τράγου; and so to 'prolong', 'linger', 'curtail' (horses, lambs, al fresco drinks, your lounging); and so to 'Lent', or similar period of restraint, when you might give up luggage, bucket lists, look gorgons in the face and find—at last—your backbone

MARK EDGECOMBE

Poplar

Poplar is wind's audience, more adoring
than any host, each leaf moved
the same by the same gusts, loving and loved,
like a skiff at lake-edge mooring
tugging and slackening at lake waves' lapping.
Poplar is spine and spindling ribs, is enlarged,
enlightened yew, is honest gauge
of atmosphere, is earth's unharried clapping.
Poplar is upright, at ease and at attention
both. In company, poplar is line, is perimeter, is stand,
is all at once shambling and brahmin and grand.
Poplar is mighty, unrequiring mention,
spire-like, greenly steepling, sufficiently meek
and strong as not to mind appearing weak.

DIANA BRIDGE

The White Colt

For Vincent O'Sullivan

We stayed with words that morning. You looked outwards
across oceans to places where your life and thoughts had led. I
looked back. I felt allusion open—yet, for all the talk of China,
there was nothing to remind me that millennia ago,
the sage came up with this: *Man's life between heaven and earth
is a white colt passing a crack in a wall—suddenly it's gone.*

The line is like a diamond, as bright as it is incontestable.
You would have felt its reach, the dizzying scale of heaven and earth
and, taking place between, our brief unstable lives.
It was never a crutch for a man to lean on; you would, like me,
have shivered at the narrowness of the gap the flying hooves
traverse as they drum it out, the shortness of our span.

You loved words that skim the edge of the imagination,
that catch as they heighten fact. On that unclouded morning
we might have sat and relished it, the sage's version
of the oldest truth; and then gone on to marvel at the way
the white, high-stepping colt eclipses the bleak truism
that called it into life. The line went unrecalled.

There was nothing to alert us, nothing at all to warn
that a life was hurtling past. You were one
who faced the facts. In the days that followed, I fancy
that you would have looked the white colt in the eye
and later held the line the way one does a piece of jade, half
charm, half consolation, as you entered your fifth act.

SIMON RICHARDSON

A Slow Act

1. *Vincent O'Sullivan*, 2022, egg tempera and gold leaf on panel, 520 x 600mm, Kirk Collection.
2. *Mila and Hot Water Bottle*, 2022, egg tempera and gold leaf on panel, 310 x 330mm, Kirk Collection.
3. *Woman in a Blue Blanket*, 2021, egg tempera on panel, 330 x 320mm, Private Collection.
4. *Jeffrey Harris*, 2023, egg tempera and gold leaf on panel/wood, 660 x 625mm, Ballin Collection.
5. *Fiona Pardington*, 2024, egg tempera on panel, 650 x 560mm, private collection.
6. *Jeffrey Harris*, 2022, egg tempera on panel, 340 x 345 mm, Kirk collection.
7. *Grahame Sydney*, 2024, egg tempera and gold leaf on panel, 660 x 550mm, Ballin Collection.
8. *Mila and Tontu*, 2023, egg tempera and silver leaf on panel, 265 x 240mm, Private Collection.

One of my favourite parts of editing *Landfall* is corresponding with artists and selecting the work that will feature in each issue. When I took on the editorship, one of the first artists I reached out to was Simon Richardson. In 2020, Simon told me that he was working on some portraits but that he works slowly. Several years later, I saw his portrait of Vincent O'Sullivan in the flesh, on the wall of Vincent's house in Port Chalmers; a quiet presence, his portrait loomed almost as large as the person himself. When Vincent died earlier this year, Simon agreed for this portrait to feature on the cover.

    Simon's work is glacially slow. In these portraits, the viewer can see the fruits of this arduous labour—meticulous detail, beguiling complexity and an extraordinary articulation of light and shadow. In the many, many hours spent looking, contemplating, interrogating, Richardson has seen and held—psychoanalytically speaking—the essential spirit housed in the bodies of those in his portraits. In the slow act of looking, Richardson offers us a radical antidote to the contemporary disposition: attentiveness, persistence, presence. And, above all, sheer craft; *perfected attention*, as Vincent might say.

—Lynley Edmeades

MICHAEL D. JACKSON

Vincent

Vincent O'Sullivan was a year or two ahead of me at Auckland University, and we did not meet until after I'd published a poem in a student magazine called *Outline*, whereupon Vince got in touch and generously invited me to show him some of my work-in-progress. *Il miglior fabbro*, he not only provided me with meticulous critiques, pointing out an image that did not ring true, muddled syntax and slipshod prosody; he gave me the kind of encouragement that makes all the difference when one is writing blind.

What satisfaction did Vincent get out of mentoring me? I suppose it was the same sense of relief that I felt realising that I was not labouring alone in what Dylan Thomas called our 'craft and sullen art'. Slowly, we warmed toward each other as people, not just poets, and became fast friends. I was a fool for his mordant wit and irreverent humour, and envied him his fund of stories and literary wisecracks culled from Oscar Wilde, the Smith of Smiths, and of his run-ins with bullshit artists. Here was a man with the gift of the gab, as they say. Someone who could talk his way out of a paper bag and bring a smile to the face of a clock.

The same year my first poem appeared in print, I went south to a University of New Zealand arts festival in Dunedin. Among the many bohemians, beatniks and luminaries I met that winter was a Greek-New Zealand poet called Antigone Kefala (who went on to study French literature at Victoria University before moving to Australia in 1960, where she published several books of poetry and a poignant memoir of her Wellington childhood called *Alexia: A tale of two cultures*). Mindful of Vince's classical background and affection for all things Greek, I lost no time in telling him about Antigone. Entranced by the name, as I fully expected him to be, Vincent wrote a poem in which he conjured his own Antigone, a synthesis of the classical figure and a woman entirely of his own imagining.

In Dunedin I also met Charles Brasch, editor of *Landfall*. Brasch showed an interest in my poetry and invited me to send him some of my work. When one of my poems was accepted for publication I urged Vincent to submit something of his, hoping we could make our Landfall debuts together. So it was that his 'Antigone' and my 'To Be Hanged by the Neck' both appeared in the December 1959 issue, our first significant forays into print.

Even at this early stage, Vincent had found his voice. In 'Antigone' one can pick up the vernacular ellipses and idioms of New Zealand speech, a measure of the author's commitment not only to unpretentiousness but to the ways in which the miraculous finds expression within the mundane. His poems are epiphanies, life constantly taking him by surprise—'a woman folding curtains as she leaves/ a man, forever', and 'The smile that opens simply as a dove's wings/ and what is in flight is everything, is everything'. This recognition of the exotic in the quotidian is part of what drew Vincent to John Mulgan, in whom, however, the struggle between an educated sensibility and a strong identification with the common man was never fully resolved. In Vincent's biography of Mulgan he remarks that Mulgan was at home among men who earned their living with their hands, and with women who were straightforward and practical. He liked playing darts and cards with country people, and drawing out old soldiers to tell him how it was before the peace they fought for. He was not bothered by hierarchies or status or intellectual attainments. Directness, the importance of not posturing, taking people on their own terms, were coming to define for him the good side of being a New Zealander.[1]

Though modesty would forbid it, Vincent might well have been describing himself here.

★

During the sixty years that have passed since Vincent and I first met we have found ourselves living in the same place at the same time on only a couple of occasions. Most of our conversations have been during flying visits, brief sojourns, in which we have had to work hard to catch up on news while recounting tall stories about old acquaintances, recalling old times, discussing our writing and, more recently, mourning the deaths of mutual friends.

Both of us have been haunted by the difficulty of reconciling our strong identification with our homeland with an equally strong sense of being a part of a European tradition of thought, of literature, and of political critique that, for all its importance to us, was paradoxically not a part of our upbringing but something we adopted and made our own. Sometimes this tension finds expression in geographically disparate images, as in Vincent's Central America poems, his numerous poems about Greece, both modern and classical, his sonnet sequence on Charles Meryon, the famous French etcher who lived for a while in Akaroa, or his play about Japanese prisoners-of-war in the Wairarapa; sometimes it shows as a tension between the colloquial banter of, say, Butcher and Baldy, and the 'sweet high figure/ inside every butcher' that is momentarily illuminated as a redneck lights a cigarette against the wind, 'his hands cupping a match/ like a yellow stone'. Vincent visits Yeats' grave on the day a bomb destroys an innocent boy. He takes a fatally wounded thrush from the mouth of his cat. Plato appears among the cockatoos. These incongruities are grist for the poet's mill. But the poet does not seek any moral resolution, for the sparks that fly from these juxtapositions are what make poetry both necessary and illuminating. 'There is something like the glint of a hook,/ there is something, love, in that shimmering/ vault, trolling too fast to speak of.'

★

One day in January 2003 I visited Vincent in the Wairapapa—a region that the legendary Haunui-a-Nanaia named at the end of an epic journey in pursuit of his runaway wife, Wairaka, when he glimpsed from the ridge of the Remutaka Range the glint of sunlight on the waters of the lake. I too was searching for something at this time—something that had got away from me, and without which my life felt tenuous and unresolved. Was it nostalgia for the place in which I had lived my most formative years? Not exactly, because it was not the past I pined for. If anything, I wanted to live in two places at once—Aotearoa and Elsewhere—much as some men want both a wife and a mistress. But despite the bumper-sticker injunction 'Think globally, act locally' it is simply not possible to *live* both locally and globally. We cannot be somewhere and everywhere at the same time, though we can, I imagine, think of ourselves as being someone and everyone at the same time.

Vincent had just published his biography of Mulgan, and it had inspired me to reread the posthumous *Report on Experience*, which Mulgan referred to as only a 'draft and outline of a book I'd like to write'. He speaks of New

Zealand in ways that were immediately familiar to me, having just flown in from Sydney on a gusty, rainswept day, the sea cutting up rough beneath our wings, and wooden houses clustered together on the hills like lost sheep. Mulgan says that we New Zealanders—which is to say Pākehā New Zealanders—have always been too few and far between to have had the confidence needed to make the country truly and deeply our own. And so we are restive, and live as strangers, he says, and go abroad *looking not for adventure but for satisfaction*.

When he took his own life in Cairo in April 1945, only twelve days before the peace, Mulgan seems to have felt it would be as impossible for him to find satisfaction in the New Zealand he had known as a young man as it would be to find it in the Oxford he had known before the war. In no-man's land, oppressed by the contradictions of his war experiences in Greece, where every successful partisan raid had meant immediate German reprisals against the very villagers who had sheltered and befriended his men, and where, even as he wrote his last messages, a brutal civil war, abetted by England, was tearing Greece apart, he chose oblivion.

As Mulgan's fate suggests, the question as to where one belongs is clearly, and painfully, related to the question of to whom is one beholden. Like his friends and contemporaries, Jim Bertram, Geoffrey Cox, Ian Milner and Jack Bennett, it was not enough to be a New Zealander; one was inescapably part of a wider world in which one had to take a stand, in which one was obliged to act. Vincent observes of these men of Mulgan's generation:

> The sense of contending pressures could generate a peculiar malaise of its own. As Thomas Norrington, an Englishman who knew and worked closely with several of them, concluded in retrospect, there seemed an innate melancholy in the New Zealanders he knew.[2]

That Vincent did not succumb to this malaise, this melancholy, attests to his genius in holding in tension traditions, idioms and mores that only a generation ago were regarded as anathema to each other. He gave New Zealand letters a maturity and audacity it lacked for a long time. He blazed a trail, took extraordinary risks and lived a charmed life, his saving grace his unfailing sense of humour, his uncanny sense of what is true and what is not, and his devotion to his friends.

That Wairarapa day we were in an ebullient mood, sharing reminiscences at a table in the shade of some fruit trees with Vincent's wife Helen and his son Dominic. It was very hot. The hills were like loaves of bread, dusted with flour, the sky deep cobalt, with curious tufts of unmoving cloud, as if painted by a hyperrealist. Vincent and I were piecing together details of a weekend in late 1965 when he and his first wife, Tui, drove up from Wellington with Les and Mary Cleveland and stayed with me in the Wairarapa. I was teaching at Kurunui College at the time, and towards the end of that year had rented a schoolhouse in Featherston so that my girlfriend, who was completing her final year at Victoria University in Wellington, could join me for the summer.

I recounted to Vincent, Helen and Dominic, how, in order to get this house, I had had to pretend to have just got married. The result was an embarrassing ceremony in the staffroom one morning, at which I was presented with His and Hers bath towels and toiletries, and given the loan of a car so that my new 'wife' and I could explore the Wairarapa. I remembered us drinking ouzo at Morrisons Bush hotel; Vincent remembered us in the pub at Lake Ferry one day, and a trip to the Pinnacles …

But I should let Vincent have the last word.

In his exquisite essay *On Longing* he reminds us that, for a child, reality is at once the world at hand *and* the worlds of which one dreams.

> What is so living and graspable and immediately there in front of you and what is quite as real but you will never touch—the Seven Swans of Glendalough or whatever the other stories are that you hear; and that place the grown-ups talked of, the enchanted distance where they were young, that you so desperately want to know as well. That gap where for many of us longing begins.[3]

Notes
1. Vincent O'Sullivan, *Long Journey to the Border: A life of John Mulgan* (Penguin, 2003), pp. 78–89.
2. Ibid., p. 115.
3. Vincent O'Sullivan, *On Longing* (Four Winds Press, 2002), pp. 9–10.

CINDY BOTHA

flood

you can't envision it
until the river's muscle, full of rain
becomes personal
high-water marks accelerate
up bookcases and linen cupboards
the ceiling fan
a rudder, still vacillating

the water you imagined
clear as tides is mud-dull and foul
debris anarchic
as nunchucks and flick knives
the spate defeats sofas
launches double beds

and when, days later, it drains away
offloading its tonnage
of silt and sludge
all the electrics are wrecked
the orchard's gone
and the old tired dog
is drowned in his kennel

HANNAH PETUHA

The Halo Effect

I first met Neve at a house party in Mount Maunganui. She was tall, blonde and tanned. An influencer typecast. She wore a string of pearls and a shell necklace that sat around her collarbones, and a silk dress that barely passed her crotch. Her hair was in tight curls—I couldn't figure out if they were natural or artificially crisp—and her lips were an iridescent shade of gloss that glimmered like the surface of a tide pool, so of course when she asked what I did I said—

'Water.'

'Hm?' she said.

'Sorry?'

'What do you do?'

'Oh,' I said. 'I'm kinda between jobs at the moment.'

Truthfully, I was working at a kiwifruit packhouse in Te Puke, where I lived, but the lie was habitual and it was more relatable to say you were unemployed. Unemployment was in.

Neve put down her Aperol Spritz and the ice chattered. She flashed her inner forearm and I saw a small ribbony bow tattoo at her wrist. It's funny, the things I remember.

'I get that,' she said. 'Job searching is super hard at the moment.'

I nodded.

'Do you live around here?' she asked.

'Yeah.'

It was easier to say I was from the Mount. The Mount was lush. The Mount was the Mediterranean beach of the Southern Hemisphere. The Mount was peak tourism. The Mount was all gym bros and yoga pants. The Mount was where K.J. Apa was spotted on holiday in 2017 and the town went crazy. The Mount was *the* Mount.

In response, people always told me the Mount was so pretty and I was so lucky to live here, so I'd indulge them saying: Yes it's really nice, and yes I have a flash house you can stay in, I know the best coffee stalls and restaurants, and yes I wake up early to go for morning swims, yes in the evenings I run up the Mount, yes I can surf, no I'm not that good but I can stand up on a board, yes I know I'm so lucky I'll live here forever!

I thought if I lied enough my lies would eventually become self-fulfilling, but not all things back then worked out the way I hoped.

'Yeah,' Neve said. 'I'm from Auckland but I moved here a few weeks ago. I've always wanted to and I'm so glad I did. It's so nice here.'

'Yeah,' I said. I slackened into my plastic mould and smiled. 'So nice.'

⋆

In the party bathroom I searched her up on Instagram. Her handle was the first to come up: @neveintheleaves:

130 posts

3487 followers.

Her feed was filled with her recent holiday in Spain, modelling for local Mount Maunganui clothing brands, film photos of pink sunsets and poetry about mermaids. *Water me in my ocean, moana, moana, moana.* I didn't get it. I clicked on a reel of her swimming, her bow tattoo rippling underwater like a piece of seaweed tangled around her wrist.

I clicked Follow from my auto-generated account—Quinceañeralover134—and felt a rush of dopamine. After the party was over, continually refreshing my home page for several days, I never got a follow back.

⋆

The weeks after went more or less like this: I worked a shift in the packhouse, throwing kiwifruit from conveyor belts into bins. On my way out I blew a kiss to the Kiwi 360 monument. At home I'd turn on my laptop to watch Netflix, then remember my laptop was broken. My trailer was a cramped room that backed onto the motorway and the shuddering of logging trucks and trains lulled me to sleep. I'd wake up. I'd check Neve's Instagram.

I decided I'd drive to the Mount every weekend. I parked in a parking lot behind a Botox clinic, put on a cap and sunglasses and strolled. I walked down the streets, past the odd café and the surfboard rental shop. All the houses looked like Hollywood sets. Palm trees and blue skies. Wraparound balconies with views of the Pacific Ocean. Tennis courts and private pools. Artificial lawns with water sprinklers. I could picture myself in all of them, sprawled on a tanning bed, a magazine sitting on my chest as I lapped up the sun. I'd always wished I'd been born into that kind of life.

At the beach I checked Instagram and clicked on Neve's story. It was an image of her apartment view. I recognised the location instantly. She lived in one of those blocks that faced Pilot Bay and the harbour bridge. In the story, white yachts freckled the ocean. I screenshotted it and clicked. The next story was of her at brunch with a friend in a café not too far from where I was—posted fifteen minutes ago. I walked off the beach and onto Main Street until I was one store away from the café.

There was Neve, sitting outside with her back to me. Her hair was in the same crisp curls, her top had a low back that exposed three moles dotted down her spine. For a second I felt awful. A guilt complex rose in me, telling me off for following her all the way there, standing a few metres away, watching her. I shook it off. I wasn't stalking; I was just interested. I was curious.

I pressed my sunglasses up my nose and walked past as she drank her coffee, flicking through her Instagram. I remember smiling then, feeling a rush of adrenaline, purely for the idea of Neve looking up from the table and noticing me. I imagined her face illuminating with recognition and familiarity, an affirmation that I had the kind of face that was memorable, the kind of face that makes a stranger seem trustworthy. I kept that image of her in my mind and didn't look back. I crossed the road and headed to my car.

★

Every weekend I parked behind the Botox clinic and walked around, checking Neve's Instagram every five minutes. It was the start of summer and pōhutukawa flowers bloomed around the base track of the Mount. On my walks I loved looking out to the blue horizon. I loved how hazy it was, like looking into a dream. When I was a kid, I thought I could sweep the whole ocean up in my plastic tea cup and drink it in one gulp. I felt the same way every time I looked out.

And every weekend there was a new story. I remember one particularly well. The photo showed her tanning at Main Beach, lying on a checkered beach towel. I changed my route instantly, speed-walking around the Mount down to the beach, trudging through volleyball games and families until I spotted her. I kept my distance. The sand, boiling hot, seared my bare feet.

Neve was lying down with her earphones in. She had a kind of shimmery moisturiser lathered over her whole body. The breeze picked up and I caught a sweet fragrance of coconut and vanilla which I was sure came from her. Whatever moisturiser she used, I wanted it. I stood with my eyes closed to take in her scent, her gleaming presence. When I opened my eyes she'd rolled over onto her stomach and adjusted her earphones. Her towel flapped in the breeze.

★

I had an online boyfriend once. He was called Brian and was from New Jersey, and when we FaceTimed he always had dollops of mayonnaise in the corners of his mouth. He'd take me on online dates and change our FaceTime backgrounds—Maccas, Burger King, the Statue of Liberty, Chipmunks—we'd been to them all. I didn't talk much, I was just happy that I had a boyfriend. I was happy to let him speak his mind while I clipped my toenails.

'Hot people are just so privileged,' he said once. 'They date and marry other hot people and they have hot kids, and they keep repopulating the world that way.'

He often said those kinds of things and really meant them. It made his rosacea flare up. I always nodded. To be honest I agreed with him. Good-looking people had no idea how lucky they were. They had no idea what it was like to be ugly.

I knew from a young age I was different—not in a special way, like being a princess or destined for fame being able to control people with your mind—but different in the sense of repulsiveness. I knew, while looking at the shapes and folds of my face in the mirror, that I would not be a winner. I knew I wasn't a child with looks and I wouldn't grow into them. As I got older I knew this was the reason I never had friendships, I didn't have a good enough face. People only ever described me as *nice*—a translation of nondescript, or all right, that small degrading phrase.

So I grew up spending my spare time reading articles that criticised celebrities, ones that revealed they were actually nepo babies or had trust funds or were drug addicts. I loved seeing candid photos of them snapped at the worst times, looking like they'd just woken up from an overdose or with their stomach hanging out of their crop tops.

I liked the idea that no matter how they presented themselves, for a second they could feel how it felt to be me. But I was also still so jealous of them, their effortless good looks and how easy their lives looked in their social media posts. None of them knew what it was like to live alone in a trailer and work in a kiwifruit packhouse. I hated them for that.

Sometimes while FaceTiming my boyfriend I'd let him talk and talk while I cut out magazine pictures of Margot Robbie and James Marsden, and patted their hair and whispered in their ears about how much I loved them and wanted them to die, and twirled them around my room, taped together paper people.

When I watched Neve, these feelings came back to me and I weighed them over like a sand timer, both admiring and despising her and wishing I lived in any body except my own.

★

Another notification: a brunch. I stood on Main Street where I saw her with a dozen other people cheersing drinks. I watched from behind a pair of folded-down umbrellas. They took photos of each other on their disposable film cameras. They talked and ate and laughed and swirled the straws in their fishbowls.

The sun peaked and the group slowly dispersed. I watched them leave in small groups until Neve got up and walked in my direction. I tilted my head down as she passed. She was barefoot and had dark tan lines from her Birkenstocks. I waited until she was a safe distance ahead and followed.

She cut through a few streets, whistling to herself and looking up at the sky. I remember how cloudless the day was and the salt tang that sprinkled the air. We ended up on the street of her apartment block; I stopped a few metres away as she approached the building. I watched her take out her swipe key and enter the lobby. The door shut behind her.

A few minutes later I got another notification: It was a view of her flat balcony from the lounge, captioned: *Join me for live yoga in 15*.

I waited outside the lobby trying to look inconspicuous, taking my cap into my folded arms, tapping my feet. Soon enough a guy in jandals was on his way out of the building.

'Did you wanna go through?' he asked, holding the door slightly open for me.

'Yeah, thanks,' I said casually. I walked through the door and heard it seal shut behind me.

I was met with fresh aircon and lemon antiseptic. The lobby was quiet. My hands trailed over the cool counter top, bench and walls as I approached the elevator. I hopped in and looked at the numbers. I took a wild guess, pressed Level 3 and was swiftly raised up, the doors opening to a pristine hallway. At the end was a large window with a view of the harbour bridge.

It was impossible to know which apartment was Neve's. I peered through each door's peephole but could make out nothing. I was near the end of the hallway when I heard someone inside a room approach their door and saw the handle slowly turn. I was in front of the emergency exit. I dipped out.

The exit led out to a flat ledge and a flight of stairs. Instinctively I walked down, and to my left were windows looking into various people's lounges. A family room, one with hippy tapestries of psychedelic elephants, and then I saw it—the view that matched all the screenshots on my camera roll.

It was what you'd expect Neve's flat to look like. The lounge wall was lined with prints of bright flowers in vases. A record player sat on a wicker table. A large wall poster read: *Have you ever had a bad time in the 70s?* which I remember Neve at the party saying was her favourite decade.

'Because of the misogyny?' I'd asked.

'What? No,' she said. 'I like everyone's clothes from that era—and the music.'

'So, not because of the political activism? The Polynesian Panther Party?' She laughed.

A yoga mat was on the floor. A plate of incense was burning. I peeked a little further over the railings and saw a door half open to another room. Neve walked in through it. I ducked and crouched on the stairs. The railings were a stainless steel block design with tiny holes through which I could see the top half of her lounge. I could hear her through the open window. Even her footsteps sounded like glitter. She connected to her Bluetooth speaker and music played. I could envision Neve right then: a tripod set up to film her yoga on the mat, a downward dog through the haze of incense.

★

When I broke up with my boyfriend I wanted to change my life, quit my job, uproot everything and move countries. I bought an online mentorship programme that helped you look at different career options—an entrepreneur, an investor, that type of crap. I couldn't get any service from my trailer so I ended up in a dingy all-night café on my failing laptop, reading all the booklets and listening to impersonal five-minute clips about meritocracy and determination. I remember being tired and felt my attention waning. My focus shifted from what was on the screen to my blue-light reflection. If I squinted, all my features disappeared, like a ghost.

★

I was on the stairs for what felt like forever. The sun lowered. My body was starting to cramp up and I felt twinges in my hamstrings. I changed into a kneel, which gave me a better view into Neve's lounge. I saw her there on the yoga mat, her arms stretching up to the roof and the curls on her heart-shaped head and her big brown eyes that blinked and turned to the window and looked at me.

'What the fuck?'

I ducked. Her music turned off. She walked to the window.

'Is someone out there?'

I slowly shuffled up towards the emergency exit wall so I was hidden.

'Creep!' she shouted. 'Just so you know, I've got you on video. I can take it to the police!' She shut her window.

I sat behind that wall, paralysed. I had a new viewing angle now—the small back window of someone's toilet. On the sill there were several seashells piled together and a stack of off-brand toilet paper. *Save the world, wipe with us!* the wrapping said. Then someone flushed.

After an hour I tried the exit door but it was locked. I listened for signs of life. No music, no glitter footsteps, so I slowly began crawling down the stairs until I reached the emergency ladder. I climbed right down and landed between rows of large rubbish bins. I adjusted my cap and stealthily made my way back to the car, only to find the park empty. There was a new sign drilled into the wall: *Reserved Parking. Towaway Applies.*

I walked to the bus stop, fumbling in my pocket for some change. The afternoon was warm and the mirage rippled across the bitumen. A bus rolled up. I took one last look in the direction of Neve's apartment before hopping on.

The Mount got smaller and smaller in the bus's wing mirror until it was a green speck behind the motorway. I went on Instagram and Neve had posted a story: *I'm sick and tired of weirdos trying it out and thinking they can invade my personal space. Fuck off! If anyone recognises this perv, let me know.* The caption was above a blurry picture of me on the emergency stairs. You couldn't tell it was me though, not with the cap and sunglasses. It could've been anyone.

I went out of Instagram. I turned off my phone and my reflection flickered on the screen. It slowly slid away from me, through my fingers, onto the bus floor.

HOLLY FLETCHER

No Solutions for your Illness

The man selling goji berries was trying to call the house again. He let the phone ring eleven times before hanging up. He claimed to have the answer for the sickness that was consuming you. But really, he was just porridge. The same way your jumper with all its creamy crevices covered your slighting body. The berries talked big with their night shadowy mouths. But they couldn't hide the dying.

I was making links to pull you ashore, but you were already on the horizon of this world. Why weren't you eating? How could we have been so deaf to what was coming? There is so much importance on the breath and you're forgetting this now as it shallows. Poetry cheapens you, the birds outside know nothing. We wait until the ringing stops. Our faces suspended around you, like paper party plates. Our distorted features drawn on with crayon. But they couldn't hide the dying.

HEIDI BRICKELL

A koru is a trajectory

Mixed media installation, 2024, Enjoy Contemporary Art Space.
All photographs by Cheska Brown.

A koru is a trajectory is a collaboration between Heidi Brickell and the whenua, moana and ngā atua Māori. The materials used in this exhibition explore the relationship between Tangaroa and Tāne Mahuta—atua of the sea and forest. Through her practice, Brickell reinforces her bonds to her tūpuna, te taiao and Te Moana-nui-a-Kiwa. Rākau from Ōtaki, sanded by Tangaroa, is lovingly twined with hand-dyed cotton in shades of blue, green and purple, resulting in contorted sculptural forms that embody the relationship between sea and land. They are connected to spirals, anthropomorphic forms and twisted masses made from rimurapa. Varying in colour and size, these works are suspended from Enjoy's ceiling at different heights. Some are encircled in twined wire, while others have straight rods pierce right through them. Kōhatu and smaller rākau connected to certain works are grounded on the gallery floor using vertical threads. Most works feature koru—*the* defining motif of toi Māori. Much more than symbolising new life, Brickell considers how the koru form that pervades mātauranga Māori is the fundamental shape of physics that our bodies have learned to weather. Arranged in sequences that allow visitors to weave in between artworks, the artist transforms the gallery to reflect the rimurapa ngahere in the moana that are in steady decline. A koru is a trajectory reflects the alarming environment that we live in while simultaneously exemplifying the ways that we can honour it.

—Brooke Pou (Ngāpuhi, Ngāi Te Rangi)

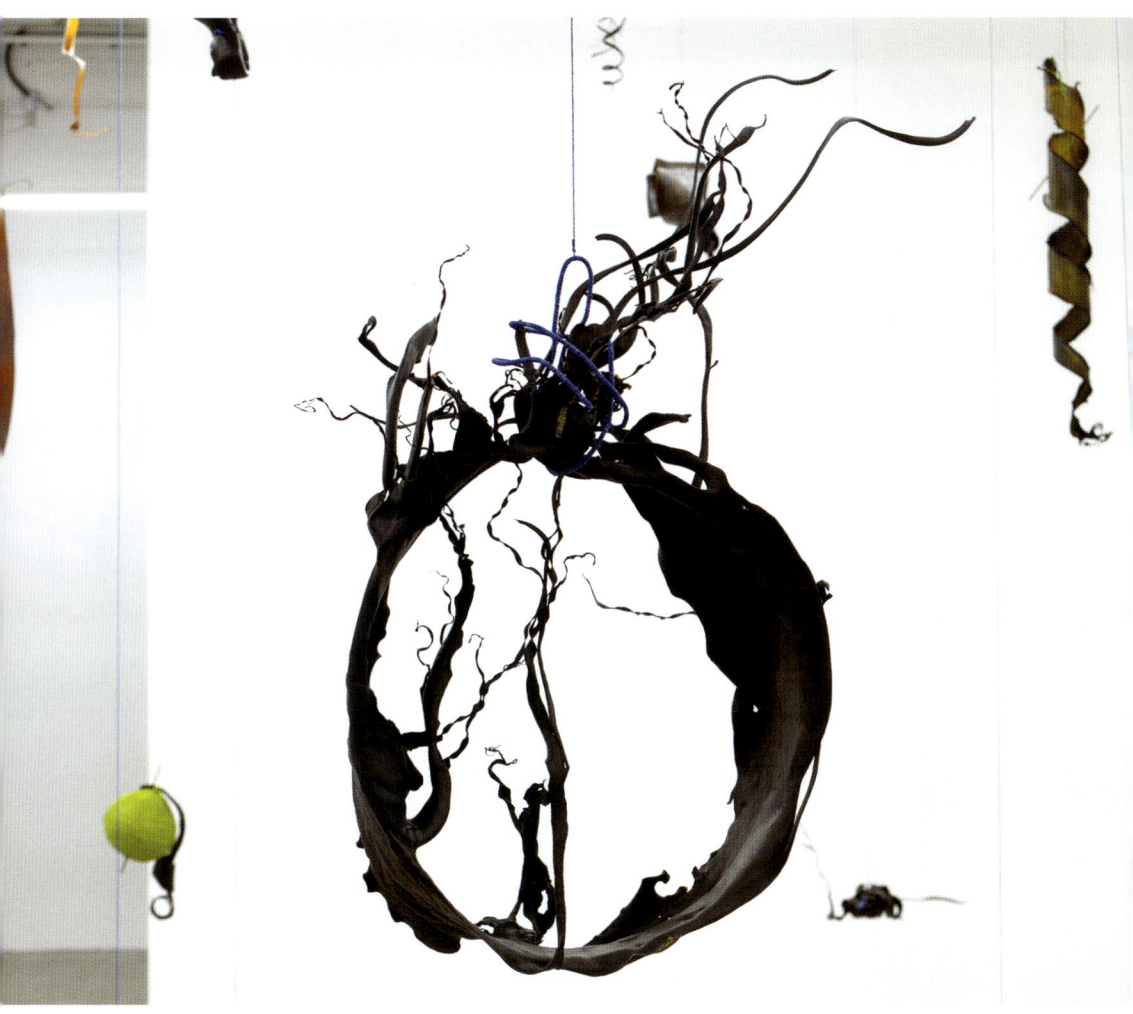

DAVID EGGLETON

The Arisen

You're cussing Big Bang theology,
rising to the power of X.
You're tethered to a balloon,
rising in some necessary way.
You're old and looking leathery,
with rising visible scars.
You're rising with hurt feelings,
and unsafe trigger words.
On the internet, no one knows
you're not an April Fool rising.
The Milky Way is your vortex,
rising above a Matariki nation.
Whiskerandoes, rising from their Harleys,
slurp from wellness bowls.
A chequered flag mosaic is rising,
to sweep down for the win.
So put a ring around that sinkhole,
let it take you out to the ocean,
there where a righteous whale is rising
to blow some rock and roll.

PHILIP TEMPLE

7 October 2023

Down hot streets the tourists flow and slow
searching for the best gelato.

Santa Maria Novella cool,
the pews and cushions ready.
The priestly scent is wedding white roses.
In nómine Patris, et Fílii, et Spíritus Sancti.

A shrine supplicant, bob cut,
stares at Mary and Jesus crowned,
dreaming of candle-lit virgin birth.

Students at the table in San Marco
talk briskly of Donatello.

There are festivals abroad
to satisfy the bored or burnt,
the sound of desert screams
of ravers, songs never learnt.

Down hot streets the tourists flow and slow
searching for the best gelato.

TONY BEYER

Clearance

no one else seems to notice
or particularly mind
bare dead branches appealing to the sky
out of a mound of gathered soil

the rest of the garden is a wasteland now
flattened by caterpillar tracks
the metal sort not those soft multiple feet
programmed for metamorphosis

a steel barrier fence
emphasised by signage has replaced
the overgrown front hedge
which only ambiguously forbade entry

an occasional bird
perches on one of the lifeless twigs
and preens then darts like the ghost of itself
somewhere beyond sight

at night it's as if the trees
and the former house still remain
under stars that stirred above them
all the time they were there

MEDB CHARLETON

Awakening

Along convolvulus-ridden hedgerows
I walked in the mending sun,
Past fields that took off for a quick bloom,
Light blazing through long grasses.
There I leaned in likenesses listening
To wildflowers' standing ovations,
To concordance, emergence, brevity,
And the wind, making music in farm iron.

FRANKIE McMILLAN

Separation

You can talk to the cow. Lay your cheek against her flank, position the bucket and, oh cow, you say, another blooming morning, another blooming day, and you reach under the warm bulk of her, you grasp her full teats in your hands. You, ready, cow? Outside the trees stir, crankiness in the air, a flight of starlings over the barn. Soon the sun will light up the iron roof, blaze through the slats. Soon the calf will stop calling.

You can talk to the cow. About missing things. Your keys to the locked cupboard. Your boy. Where is he, you say, where did he go? The cow shifts in her stall. Her horns lightly toss the hay. Your feet grip the bucket tighter. Steady, cow. She turns her head. Blinks when you talk to her about missing things. Outside leaves gather, crisp as brown shirts. You talk about how the brown shirts scuttle across the field. How they mound up in piles, so deep a small boy can bury himself up to his neck. You can talk to the cow, even as her milk sprays out into the bucket. Even as it spills out over your wrist. The cow bellows. I know, cow, you say. I know.

ANNA WOODS

The Years

YEAR ONE   They are always together. His hand pressing into hers, pulling her towards him when a car sweeps too close, steering her by the shoulder around obstacles on the footpath—a stroller, a bicycle, a woman tying her shoelace. The concrete is broken in places and he makes sure she doesn't trip. She likes the way he opens doors for her, and the way he looks at her when he does—eyes tipped as though she's the sun. He likes her smallness. Her suppleness. The soft skin of her inner elbow, laced with veins, undoes him. The invernal sea follows them while he walks her home. Grey, silver, green. Sometimes, in the evenings, gold. This is how it begins.

YEAR TWO   She learns to cook. When they move in together it seems necessary. The kitchen is small. She stands at the blue laminate bench, overlooking the neighbour's washing line, and stares at their underwear while she peels fruit. She makes plum tarts the colour of blood. When she slices them, they have the texture of flesh. They stain her hands red. He eats the tarts unthinkingly; it doesn't occur to him the effort they take. He thinks about her all the time, while working for a boss he hates—her small, strong hands, her slender waist. His office is suffocating, the people are obtuse; he has made a mistake. She's a primary school teacher; he thinks her a saint.

YEAR THREE   He brings home flowers wrapped in butcher's paper. It doesn't matter that they're pink carnations, the flowers of petrol stations and hospital gift shops; she puts them in the tallest glass they own—she must buy a vase she thinks, then forgets each time—until the broken heads drop to the floor. There's an art to arranging them, her mother says, but she never learned it. It's difficult to remember to replace the water. When she catches sight of them her heart stretches against the bars of her chest. He can't say why he brings them, it's just something you do. He would bring her the world if he could. When her face splits with surprise, it's enough.

YEAR FOUR   He works late in the city, at a job he doesn't yet understand, for a saturnine boss who plagues him. Most days she sneaks away from school after three, spending evenings and weekends planning and marking, printing and laminating, cutting fabric and card to pin to the classroom walls. There's a bar in the village they visit on Fridays to drink dark beer, where a dove bursts from a stained-glass window. It reminds him of church as a child, the way the angled light cut the gloom like a revelation. Her lucent hair is a benediction. After, they go back to the house and make sloppy love between thin sheets. They mistakenly believe their dreams are the same.

YEAR FIVE   There's talk of children. There's a night when they drink several bottles of wine between them and he holds the strings of her hair as she crouches over the toilet. A day she forgets to bring the washing in. By the morning a bird has shat on his favourite shirt, leaving a green-black streak on the shoulder that remains after soaking. He doesn't mind; it's good luck, he reassures her. The laminate bench is stained, though she's stopped baking. He suggests—gently, he thinks—visiting a doctor, but her face slams shut. Each month he worries whether he should ask, but he never has to. The little stabs in her eyes tell him everything he needs to know.

YEAR SIX   There's a new job, a pay rise, a move to a bigger house with a bigger lawn for the children that do not come. Her parents give them a lemon tree in a terracotta pot. She dyes her hair. He doesn't like it—it loses its gleam. She doesn't dye it back. Sometimes she walks around the empty house while he's at work, catching cold shadows, and wonders why she's there. Sometimes he works later than necessary, stops on the way home for a drink before he can face her. It's not mentioned. They tuck it in with their silent children. People ask when they'll have babies. People always ask, but they've already learned what to leave unsaid.

YEAR SEVEN   He works late, and she's tired all the time. She stops cooking. They have takeaways most nights—Thai, Indian, Chinese, or ready meals from the deli. One night, when he arrives home late to another congealed korma, glossy oil puddling on the surface of the sweating container, they have a fierce argument. He sleeps in the spare room for a week. Neither apologises. One morning he returns his pillow to their bedroom and stuffs his sheets in the laundry, and that's that. It's easy to pretend; they are well practised now. It happens more often, his retreating to the spare room. They have a spare room of course. They have several. Because the children still do not come.

YEAR EIGHT   They holiday at a resort that serves cocktails by the pool and has a swim-up bar. She reads a book and he sleeps in the sun, getting so burnt his forehead blisters, leaving the shape of his sunglasses printed across his face like a mask for weeks. At night, lit torches glow around the resort like miniature suns. He complains about everything. She grows tired of the same deep-fried meals. The salads are limp and slimy. She develops a heat rash that dapples her skin like a pattern on fabric. A few months later she finds a bolt of fabric at a shop in the village, tiny red dots sprayed across chiffon, and buys it on a whim.

YEAR NINE   They don't talk about the children that do not come. The room they set aside becomes a dumping ground—piles of books, ill-fitting clothes, an exercise bike, her mother's old sewing machine. It sits there for months before she teaches herself to sew, using the fabric she bought the year before. The first dress is long and billowing and flawed. She wears her pinched-seam, crooked-hemmed creation around the house. He admires her tenacity but can't see the appeal. Wouldn't it be cheaper and easier to buy clothes? He knows better than to point out the mistakes, obvious even to him. He goes on long runs but grows no fitter. They both stretch towards something that keeps snapping away.

YEAR TEN   They buy a tulip-faced puppy that drops fur all over the house and takes six months to toilet train, leaving sharp-smelling puddles in the hall. It noses wetly at her knees and follows her around, rustling under her skirts. People stop her in the street to pat it, admiring its sad full eyes. They're nothing more than an evolutionary trait, he tells her; they help dogs get attention from humans. It is not, she insists, a fur baby. Still, the puppy sleeps between them in the bed. Sometimes it wags its tail in its sleep, disturbing the covers with a rhythmic thud. It smells, too, but they don't mind. Well, he does, but knows better than to say.

YEAR ELEVEN   He sometimes doesn't come home, not going anywhere, just sleeping on the sofa in his office, waking late with a crushed neck. She notices but doesn't care, busy making elaborate dresses she never wears. She talks of quitting teaching—there's plenty of money by now, with only two of them, and other people's children no long hold any appeal, but she stays. His job bores him, too, but he stays. What else is he to do? His obscure desire for a legacy seems morbid, but he longs for a gesture towards immortality all the same. People stop asking about children. It is possible—anything is possible—but unlikely at their age. She walks the dog and doesn't complain.

YEAR TWELVE   The dog finds a slab of dark chocolate and scoffs it in a sugared hurry. They drive panicked miles to the emergency vet. It's lonely on the empty road. Their headlights tunnel the blackness while the dog whimpers in her lap. The clinic is like a hospital, double doors swinging open to admit people in scrubs. A candle burns at reception, signifying that a family is saying goodbye to a beloved pet. Their dog has its stomach pumped. They take home a fat syringe of charcoal to administer the next day. She gets up several times in the night to check on it. Is this what it's like to have a baby? He wouldn't know; he doesn't wake.

YEAR THIRTEEN   There's a work trip to Europe and she flies out to meet him for a week in Greece after. The brilliant air, the white of the buildings, the blue of the sea blind them. They eat honeyed saganaki and grilled squid and drink ouzo after every meal. At night the buildings glow like bones. They rent umbrellas and loungers at the hot pebbly beach. Everyone is tanned, as though skin cancer doesn't exist. He notices women noticing him. He likes how it feels—she looked at him that way once. She misses the dog. When they get home, the wind and rain and the shadow of the extinct volcano on their doorstep remind them of a different life.

YEAR FOURTEEN   His father dies unexpectedly. It's the first time she has seen him cry. She irons him a crisp shirt for the funeral, spending a long time making sure the creases are sharp. He reads a poem at the graveside, though he's not the poetry type. She stands with his mother a little way off, holding her veined hand. He asks his mother to come and live with them, as natural to him as the egg of the sky. She doesn't know what to say, struggling to hide her relief when his mother declines. It unscrews some part of him, this double loss. A chink opens between his ribs. Contained, though, as if split open and taped together again.

YEAR FIFTEEN   They move house. It was too big, the house they bought for the children that never came. The new house is smaller, and close to the beach. They make a habit of walking each evening, the sea a mirror reflecting their thoughts. They don't talk about his late nights, though she wonders. He deflects her attention with idle complaints. She collects pretty shells. A teetering cairn builds on the table in the entranceway, until he brings home a crystal bowl wrapped in tissue and dumps the shells in. It's not to her taste but she thanks him. She drags herself to school, he drags himself to work, as though the house has a dark gravity they cannot escape.

YEAR SIXTEEN   He is made redundant from his job and is always underfoot. He notices things and fixes them—the stuck lock on the letterbox, the peeling silicone in the shower, the creeping speckles of mould in the cupboard under the stairs. He notices her—the dresses, the shine of her hair, back to its natural colour, sprinkled now with grey. One night he holds her by the shoulders and tells her to slow down, she's missing it. Missing what? she says, rushing off on another useless errand. She wants him out of her hair. All this spare time makes him think harder about how little he will leave behind—like a fingerprint on glass, so easy to wipe away.

YEAR SEVENTEEN   His mother moves into a rest-home and cries when they sell her furniture, mopping her eyes with her vein-mapped hands. This time the question of her living with them is not raised. She buys endless bolts of fabric and wears the sewing machine out. His new job is less stressful. There's less travel, more time for hobbies like fishing. He teaches her to flounder at night with a headlamp and a net. They swim every morning in Torpedo Bay. The water is thick and dark and they slice through it like oars. After, they walk home, her hair a dripping rope, and rinse their sandy feet under the garden tap. It burns a hole in the grass over time.

YEAR EIGHTEEN   She opens a small boutique on the waterfront for the clothes she has spent years designing and sewing. It is passably successful. When women in the street wear her dresses it gives her a secret thrill. They use the money for another trip. He doesn't get sunburnt and she doesn't get heat rash. The resort is full of families and they spend most days at the adults-only pool until they see a couple a few loungers over have sex under a towel. They stick to the beach after that. The neighbours watch the dog. When they get home it runs around her in circles as though to anchor her to the spot. It doesn't notice him at all.

YEAR NINETEEN   He keeps fishing. When she runs out of ways to cook the catch, he buys her a sushi-making class for her birthday. They use heavy knives to slice petals of sashimi. They learn about tang, how the width of the knife is an extension of their hands. She eats eel for the first time. They buy a set of Japanese knives for their own kitchen. The instructor tells them you are more likely to cut yourself with a dull blade. Still, she slices herself open several times. Bright red blood, sticky on her hands. He develops the habit of stabbing the tip of the knife into the chopping board until it's fluttered with holes. They eat together again.

YEAR TWENTY   Liberated at last from its pot, the lemon tree turns from a few desultory fruit to sudden prolificacy. Orbs as big as oranges, pith a hard shell around the jewelled flesh. She makes so many jars of lemon curd she can't give them all away. One night, late spring, a super moon bursts from behind the volcano, framed in the window like an omen. It reminds her of the plum tart she learned to make back at the beginning. He never works late any more. Her hair still gleams and her dresses swish like bells when she moves. He has the urgent sense they've wasted too much time. He eats lemon curd on his toast every day.

YEAR TWENTY-ONE   She diversifies into silk scarves, screen-printed with watercolours, which accumulate in the house, hanging from chairs and sofas, lying in slippery piles on the floor. They drink champagne, toasting their relationship reaching adulthood. Tipsy, they skinny dip at Cheltenham Beach, fading bodies hidden in the moon's forgiving glow. The cold, salty water hits their skin like tiny diamonds. They shriek and splash like children, the only ones on the beach. He takes her hand in a way he hasn't in years and it's as cool as the smooth lip of a shell. His is hot to her, meaty flesh burning up. They don't remember how it feels to be young, but it must have been something like this.

YEAR TWENTY-TWO   They lose both her parents and his mother in the space of a few months. She makes a black sheath dress that hangs in the closet, holding its shape like a shed skin. There's a steel-coloured scarf she wears with it that she thinks of as a shroud. Endless arrangements must be made: flowers, finger sandwiches, tepid tea, brackish coffee. They clear out her parents' house, box towers collapsing in the garage. His mother, in a rest-home, had less to dispose of, already partially erased. The split in his ribs grows larger. The crystal bowl overflows with shells. He thinks about buying another. In the meantime she stacks new shells next to it like a row of tombstones.

YEAR TWENTY-THREE   A flood in the garage ruins the boxes from her childhood home. She sits on a stool and cries while standing water pools, stinking blackly, at her feet. He tells her she doesn't need the boxes, it's all right here, and points at his temple. She doesn't tell him memory cannot be trusted. Hers is a palimpsest, written over too many times. When he's asked to mentor a new business she laughs and says her business is new, he should mentor her. He doesn't tell her she's too irresolute to be taught. The young founder reminds him of himself. He thinks of the children they never had and wonders where they'd be now if they'd come after all.

YEAR TWENTY-FOUR   They spend more time together. A dance class—fail—he stands at the edges turning red. A supper club—success—they host dinners with their friends. The scarves multiply into an accessory line and her business expands into the shop next door. She wins a local award and wears her own design to the ceremony. An updated version of the heat-rash polkadot dress, a pale scarf at her neck. He's asked to sit on the board of the founder's company. One morning a cloud hangs over the maunga. A tapered smudge like smoke. She thinks for a moment it's erupting. He sees it too, from the ferry, and starts. They laugh about it at dinner, the wicked sunrise.

YEAR TWENTY-FIVE   The dog dies and they bury its ashes one milky night under the lemon tree. She says a few words. He brings pink carnations and they bury two velvety stems with the box. The lemon tree has leaf curl, and the thick-skinned fruit lies gnarled beneath the knotted trunk in piles. They find denuded lemons on the ground. He tells her it's possums; she doesn't believe him. She makes a lemon tart as big as a dinner plate and they eat it together. They're always together now. They could invite supper club over to finish it, but don't. After meals she brings out the tart and they pick at the sides with their forks. It lasts for days.

SHERRYL CLARK

oubliette

easy to drop a man or woman
down that hole, close the heavy
iron grate, ignore their screams.
you'd need solid stone walls
a thick wooden door to block
out the desperate cries for help.
it's hard to imagine why
you'd have one in your castle
at all, but there are plenty
of other cruelties you ignore.
peasants are eminently
expendable, you say, always
more of them breeding,
always more to break their backs
in your fields, living on hard
coarse bread and cabbage
while you feast on duck and
pheasant and deer. no incentive
for you to change now unless
one day they rise up, rakes
and pitchforks in their sweaty hands,
and throw you down that hole.
that's the problem right there—
they don't forget.

BRETT REID

Best in a Sheltered Spot

My mother's green thumb I noticed enough
to know they should be in the ground by now.
They've sat on the deck a week buffeted
by shipwrecking winds. I'll need a trowel
and a stadium cushion. From Plant Barn
cribs, cyclamen cry out for a bigger
bed, permanent digs. Today's cold but calm.
Russet leaves adorn the yard, triggering
that chapelled-hour gathering up a life
summarised by flowers and gardening.
Passed down, our giant puka holds the light,
its rounded resinous crown evergreen.
The puka's roots run deep to the Three Kings.
When repotting she would take off her rings.

ALAN RODDICK

CASELBERG TRUST INTERNATIONAL POETRY PRIZE 2024 JUDGE'S REPORT

Congratulations to the Caselberg Trust for running its poetry competition each year since 2011. Back in the day, as a Trustee, I managed the competition for a time. Later, as an occasional entrant, I shook my head at the judges' indifference to the merits of my own work.

As this year's judge I can report, as my predecessors have, that the entries were 'about' love, loss, the natural world, childhood, angst, and today's big issues, especially climate change. There were poems this year in shaped verse, free verse, sonnet form, prose poems, ballads, haiku, and the sestina. There were poems with te reo Māori and poems with Gaelic in them. Were there any made with the help of Artificial Intelligence? I hope not.

Before I sat down to read the anonymised entries, I wrote out a checklist of questions: Does this poem engage me right from the start? How well does it tell its story? Does it use the language well, and with imagination? Do the words and phrases sing? Do I want to read this poem again and again?

After reading the entries 'blind', I looked forward to learning who wrote the poems that made my shortlist. It gives me great pleasure to congratulate the winner of the 2024 Caselberg Prize, Rangi Faith, for 'The Valley Where Compassion Died', and the runner-up, in a virtual photo finish, Philip Armstrong, for 'Time of Death'.

And here are some thoughts on their poems.

'The Valley Where Compassion Died': This poem is a memorial to men who died in the Battle of Passchendaele in 1917, but the inscriptions here are not what we have come to expect on cenotaphs. Personal names, their trades and professions, their ages—these make up the first three stanzas, just four words per line; daringly, the third stanza consists of numerals only. Rhyme appears in the final verse with just one more word we never find on war memorials, a word that tolls like a bell. I found the last stanza almost unbearable to read aloud, knowing that after the first line there would be a second, and then a third, because the utterance makes the verse-form, and the stanza must be completed. I salute the writer of this poem.

'Time of Death': This poem of just fourteen lines has the concentration of a sonnet, and its final four lines are beautifully written. The subject, dying, is deeply personal, but in line eleven, the reader, too, is quietly invited to sit by the bedside for 'this business [which] is a lifetime's / work'. It is a privilege to be present.

This year, three poets are highly commended for their entries: Jeni Curtis for 'the archaeology of home', James Norcliffe for 'There's Always an Edge Here', and Sherryl Clark for 'Winds of Change'.

RANGI FAITH

The Valley Where Compassion Died

(Passchendaele, 12th October, 1917)

Tom, Ted, Percy, Jimmy,
Bert, Billy, Charlie, Alfie,
Arthur, Dave, Fred, Ernie;

labourer, telegraphist, farmer, farmer,
labourer, farmer, farmer, labourer,
teamster, teamster, farm hand, schoolteacher;

24, 21, 28, 29,
32, 21, 21, 21,
28, 27, 21, 41;

son, son, son, son,
son, son, son, son,
son, son, son, son.

PHILIP ARMSTRONG

Time of Death

In memory of Ola Roff

For a moment there was silence round the bed
and in that pause she said, using a tense
she knew she'd soon be gone from, *if
anyone asks what we did this week
you can say we waited for me to die
and it took a very long time.* That's
a knockout exit line, but turns out not
to be her last words, and not quite correct
because this business is a lifetime's
work but also instantaneous.
The days and minutes slip past as you sit
and she slips in and out of them, going
elsewhere, coming back, returning there,
sussing it out till she gets used to it.

MAKING SPACE

IN COLLABORATION WITH RMIT UNIVERSITY'S non/fictionLab

The three essays published here are the second instalment in a series of collaborative essayistic projects, where writers from both sides of the Tasman were invited to work together on the topic of 'making space'. As editors, we were interested to hear how a conversational, trans-Tasman approach might shine a light on the new wave of essays currently being written in Aotearoa and Australia and to make space in these pages for this kōrero.

    Each of the three essays presented here extends the interrogation of the theme of making space as begun in *Landfall* 247. Es Foong and Ambika G.K.R. have written a timely provocation on diasporic identity in Australasia; Sholto Buck and Stayci Taylor playfully trouble assumptions around gender and performativity; and John Kinsella and Robert Sullivan riff on 'verticality', inverting the positivity of 'making' space to query the environmental ramifications of doing so. In varying levels of experimentation, all three pieces challenge the reader to consider the essay as literary device, further exemplifying the space-making mechanism of the form itself, particularly as a site for conversation and relation.

    At a time when border regimes and isolationist politics are on the rise, collaboration feels like a quiet resistance. We extend this invitation to the reader, so that together we might continue to make space—for diversity, community and meaningful connection.

Lynley Edmeades and Brigid Magner

ES FOONG AND AMBIKA G.K.R.

Two Improvisers Walk Into a Bar

A woman walks into a dance class. She takes her sneakers off at the door, her socks sliding on the polished wooden boards. She joins the collection of half a dozen bodies spread around the room, stretching against white walls, reaching her hands towards the vaulted ceiling.

What did you visualise at the sentence, 'A woman walks into a dance class?' The Writer's practice is a visual medium. The Writer creates images for a reader to walk into. When she works **really** hard, she can sometimes make those images move. Words were intentionally omitted from the paragraph above, room left for you to fill in your own assumed details. Did you see a room full of supple bodies? Young, lithe, flexible, slim bodies dressed in lycra?

Ko te māunga _____ (my mountain is _____)
    I did my OE in my 20s. A rite of passage for all young New Zealanders. Whenever I was asked where I am from, the answer of 'New Zealand' never seemed to satisfy.
    I live near the Waitakere ranges. When I first moved to Aotearoa, Rangitoto captured my imagination. My favourite hike was Roraima. I have done the Sabarimalai pilgrimage four times. None of these mountains are really mine though.
    A quintessential British man apologised to me for his ancestors having colonised mine. A very drunk woman in Melbourne told her friends not to speak to me because I look like an Arab. A man in a pub in Sydney told me confidently I don't look like a Kiwi, and when quizzed what a Kiwi looks like, he said 'Losers, because the All Blacks lost.' A tourist I met in Peru told me he visited the Dharavi slums in Bombay, and it was clear that he cared more about the people there than they cared about themselves. A Kazakhstani colleague told me, surely India is so much better off after colonisation. A

primary school teacher got very close to my face and yelled that I was going to hell for worshipping idols. I walked away from a woman in Egypt who told me I was not from India—Indians don't have noses like mine.

I've realised the reason people want me to answer 'India' when they ask me where I'm from is so they can tell me about their experience with India, their backpacking adventure, their moral judgements about Indians, what they think Indian noses look like. It is an exhausting game to play. It's so much easier to sidestep the question.

> *A middle-aged woman walks into an improv dance class. Holding onto the doorframe, she flips her sneakers off. Her own hands join half a dozen pairs of others, some smooth and supple, some hairy and freckled, some laced with blue veins as they all stretch for the ceiling vaulted over white walls.*

You now have more context. That shorthand royalty-free stock photo image of a dance class has been fleshed out. Yet, for an essay of this nature, there are more markers that are frustratingly missing. Perhaps you've already guessed some key details by The Writer's name on the byline. But what if you hadn't seen the byline?

Ko _____ tōku ingoa (my name is _____)

I come from a patronymic culture where there is no such thing as a 'surname' passed down through generations. In most parts of India, your surname is your caste. In Tamil Nadu, India, the land of my ancestors, caste violence is still too common for comfort. To circumvent discrimination on the basis of caste, most Tamilians use their father's first name as their 'surname' or their 'initial'. Our roots and our caste are not in plain sight. For safety.

My father's name is D. Ganeshkumar. My mother was R. Jagadeeswari as a child, and became G. Jagadeeswari when she married my father. I would have been G. Ambika had I grown up in India and R. Ambika after marriage. However, when we left India, we had to choose a 'proper surname' in order to work, live, enrol in school, open a bank account. My father's name was split in two. Ganesh and Kumar. Ganesh became his first name and Kumar our family name.

I tried to drop my surname entirely. Just be Ambika. Like Rhianna, Madonna, Sridevi. But I am not quite famous enough for that. I have reclaimed some of my patronymic identity and taken the performance name of Ambika G.K.R.

When I got my first job in New Zealand, I was asked to pick a simple, easy-to-remember English name to go by. The first time someone called me Amy, I died a little and switched back to Ambika. To compensate for having a not-simple, not-easy-to-remember, not-English name, I spent years mispronouncing my own name to make it as easy as possible for English speakers to hear and pronounce.

'Am-BEE-kah' emphasis on the BEE is the English way to pronounce a three-syllable name. அம்பிகா, 'AM-bi-kah' is the Tamil way to pronounce my name. Emphasis on the AM. I wish this was a unique story to me. It's not. 'A-nand' becomes 'a-NAN-d', 'HA-ri' becomes 'Harry', 'RO-hit' becomes 'Ro-HEET'.

> *A middle-aged Chinese woman walks into an improv dance class.*

Now we may have finally got to the point. But why did The Writer feel the need to make a point? If this essay was written for an Australian audience (where The Writer lives now), it is because your 'stock photo' defaulted to the woman being white. Erasure by omission. And if The Writer was writing this for an audience in her mother country, there'd be the automatic glance at the byline to 'fill in' the picture before it could even be visualised. The usual question of 'This woman is Malay-or-Chinese-or-Indian ah?'

> *A Chinese woman walks into a bar. She makes small talk with a poet at the bar counter. Over a beer he explains her culture to her.*

The Writer changes the context now. But you have been taught now to be wary of assumptions. But also not to ask questions that might cause offence or someone to feel 'other'. Though regardless of descriptors and other identity markers, surely this scene is a trope we can recognise?

Ko _____ te awa (my river is the _____)

I grew up as an expatriate in Zambia. I lived there from age one to nearly seventeen. I grew up near the Kafue River in the Copperbelt province of Zambia. It ran through the primary and secondary schools I attended.

My schools were specially built for the expatriate workers of the Zambian copper mining company. I don't speak Bemba, Nyanja or Tonga. I never adopted the diet. I was never a local or an immigrant. I cannot claim to be Zambian.

I grew up in Kitwe, Zambia. It is where I spent most of my childhood and all of my formative years. I know how to avoid snakes in the grass. I know the difference between the bites of red and black ants. I can still smell the first rain coming to end the hot and dry season. I can close my eyes and see the African sunset from the front yard of our west-facing garden. I can taste the ripening fruit on the trees in our garden. It is written into a part of my soul.

> A Chinese woman walks into a Melbourne bar to attend a poetry performance. Ordering her beer at the bar counter, she greets an older Chinese man, a poet scheduled to perform later. He asks if she's a poet and she says yes. He then asks how she makes a living because they both know it isn't through poetry. After some more small talk, he asks her if she's Singaporean-Chinese because of her accented Mandarin. When she demurs and explains she's Malaysian-born, he delivers his thesis on why Malaysian-Chinese do not participate in the arts.
>
> It's a hackneyed argument she won't repeat because she has heard it all her life. Something about pursuing money and stability to the exclusion of all else. She realises for the first time though, that none of the canned theses applies to her. And it may not actually be because she doesn't fit the mould, but because the mould was first made by a colonial power seeking to categorise a population for industrial efficiency and political control. It is now internalised by the population because group-belonging is predicated on the existence of outsiders.
>
> The Writer has departed from image-making to haranguing the reader with her personal views on culture and politics. She is angry.

She doesn't write well in anger. The images stutter and interleave with Max Headroom-style snarky commentary. Never heard of Max Headroom? You have the internet. Look it up.

Nō _____ ahau (I am from _____)

I'm Indian in a way that I'm not Zambian or Kiwi. I never really lived in India. I left when I was one. I visited my family in India every two years for about four weeks at a time. I have never experienced the Indian monsoon, attended school there, attempted to drive a two-wheeler, never been there during a big festival. I can't speak Hindi.

I can speak Tamil more fluently than some of my cousins, without an accent. I sometimes dream in Tamil. I learned to sing Carnatic music, to dance Bharathanatyam. I wear a sari, cook like a good Indian girl. I grew up Hindu, singing bhajans, attending poojai, observing Pongal, Karthikai, Navarathri, Deepavali, Vinayaka Chathruthi, Krishna Jayanthi. The longest I have consciously lived in India was when I backpacked around India, at age twenty-eight, for six weeks.

I claim Indian as part of my identity because it's impossible to deny and not something I can hide. I'm allowed to claim it because I was born there, to Indian parents.

> *A Malaysian-Chinese woman at an Australian bar listens intently to the older man, an immigrant from China. She is smiling, nodding and asking questions at all the appropriate pauses in his monologue, even though she already knows the answers. This is what she was taught respect looks like.*

> The 'Malaysian' descriptor does not change the visual image but becomes a relevant context for the dialogue in the scene. It's a descriptor imposed upon her by her accent, profession, choice of leisure or drink.

> *A Malaysian-Chinese migrant at a tram stop stretches surreptitiously, getting ready for her dance class. Two boys in the red-and-black uniform jacket of a nearby private school whisper inaudibly except for the occasional raised word: 'Chink!' It rings quaintly in her ear, this old-fashioned insult. She wonders*

if they will ask her where she comes from. If they do, she will answer in full, then return the question like a Tupperware returned to a generous neighbour, always as full as when it was first gifted.

Ko _____ te waka (my ancestral canoe is _____)

My maternal grandmother was born in Mauritius, grew up in Sri Lanka, moved to India just before marriage and lived the rest of her life there.

My children were born in Australia. They were not eligible to be Australian citizens. They were allowed to have New Zealand citizenship, but because they were not born in Aotearoa, they will not be able to pass their citizenship to their children. I could technically claim a form of Indian citizenship for them. I wonder if they might be able to get Mauritian citizenship.

Where are my children from? Let's just put that in the 'too hard' bucket for now.

An Australian-Chinese dancer walks into an improv class. She watches the bodies around her contorted into impossible angles. She carefully follows a certain curated set of movements that look aesthetically pleasing but are not too challenging to her. The sweep of a calf, the sway of an arm, careful not to elbow another moving body. She is not improvising—but she's pretty certain that her imitation of freedom approximates the real thing just ... enough.

Ko _____ tōku iwi (my tribe is _____)

My tribe. Do you mean my caste? The thing we have tried to abolish for generations in India? The reason why patronymic culture exists and my 'surname' is a mess that I'm still untangling? You want to know my tribe so you can discriminate against me based on my caste?

I started my journey into improvised comedy nine years ago. I was a stay-at-home mum at the time and needed a space to be myself. Perhaps my tribe is Improvisers.

Sometimes I wonder if I overthink these things. Improv has taught me to hold things lightly, let things go, find the humour, find the joy. It's disposable theatre after all. Can I play with this? Can I take my improv brain and ask myself: Where am I from?

A Melbourne dancer walks into a dance class holding a takeaway cup of coffee. She sheds layers of clothing from the cold outside until she is in a simple black t-shirt and plain black gym shorts. She sniffs at the air and puts her black sweater back on. Lying down at the edge of the room, she measures the distance between her body and each of the plain white walls, then the distance between the tip of her nose and the vaulted ceiling. Finally satisfied with her exact position in the room, she considers her next move. Every gesture she makes begs the next question. She sees herself running faster and faster, through the playground behind her childhood home in Selangor. The questions like the burrs of the lalang grass, the faster she ran the more insistent the clinging. Until she would get home and turn out her socks, full of burrs waiting to be fostered into cultivated gardens to grow more weed.

Ambika: So, where am I from?

அம்பிகா: You're not supposed to ask questions in improv. Kills the scene. Make statements.

Ambika: I'm from India.

அம்பிகா: Ok.

Ambika: But I've never lived there.

அம்பிகா: You just blocked your own offer. Bad improv.

Ambika: I'm a Kiwi.

அம்பிகா: I'm a Mynah.

Ambika: You're not a proper New Zealand bird.

அம்பிகா: Says who?

Ambika: Well, you're not a contestant in the NZ Bird of the Year contest.

அம்பிகா: A bat won that contest. It's not exactly an authority on the subject.

Ambika: You're introduced, not native.

அம்பிகா: This is a terrible improv scene. We've got instant conflict, we have no relationship, we don't know where we are and we're arguing about random facts.

Ambika: Yeah, fair. Call it.

அம்பிகா: Scene.

A dancer walks into an improv dance class on the lands of the Wurundjeri peoples of the Kulin Nation. Her teacher, a white woman, asks her if she is hurt.

She shakes her head and replies that she needs a moment. Her teacher gestures gently towards a quiet space at the far end where the polished wood meets two white walls. Here, for the rest of the session, as bodies old and young, male and female and non-binary, clothed in worn cotton or fresh lycra, freshly moisturised or laced in blue veins float and slam and leap and writhe, the writer dances on the floor. Which looks for the moment like not moving except for the tears and snot trickling and leaking unbidden and unstopped. Which looks for the moment like tears speaking for words she no longer knows how to write, descriptors and adjectives falling over themselves like Jenga blocks.

When there is a lull in the activity of the room, as the class takes a rest break, The Dancer-Writer moves to the centre of the room. Starting in a crouched position, she slowly starts to spin. Faster and faster, limbs swinging from her centre as the words spin away, one after another, until she is nothing but body and motion, skin and fat and bone, essence, no image, no sound, no self.

Ko Tāmaki Makaurau ahau e noho ana.
Nō Īnia ōku tīpuna.
Ko தமிழ் tōku reo.
Ko அம்பிகா tōku ingoa.

Here we are two immigrant women from the late 20th century. Products of the post-colonial upheaval and migration out of Asia and to 'the west' (technically, we travelled east). But before that, migration driven by mass starvation, escape from the traditions that bound us by foot or caste. First generation immigrants borne from generations of immigrants before them. Two vastly different trajectories if seen on a map of the world, but what we have in common is the experience of being 'in-between'. Both the 'other' and not.

We talk endlessly about the travellers that preceded us. What does history tell us about our foremothers? What were their lives like? What were their journeys about? Did they integrate into their new societies? What have they passed down to us other than their genes? We are the mark they left on the world.

We cannot answer these questions. The history of our foremothers is not widely documented—the history of Asian women, even less so. We make educated guesses, find assurance in the things we do instinctively.

Their stories, while not written, have been passed down orally, through the mother wound, the childhood traumas, through open-hearted conversations with others in the same boat, through performance art: poetry, dance, drama, comedy.

What about our own barely documented lives? The even less documented lives of countless other women who have similar, parallel stories?

Karma is said to take seven generations to resolve itself. All inflicted trauma and all healing takes seven generations to work its way through a family, village, city, country. So many moments, so many actions, so many words, so many feelings, so many microaggressions, so many laughs, so many joyful memories, so many ghosts. These live in our psyche for seven generations. Perhaps that is more powerful than having them written in a book of facts?

The process of improv is unscripted dance or dialogue. In order to show up, we have to be prepared to let go of our ideas and simultaneously hold our points of view. We want to create a safe space for the audience, the perceivers of our art, in order to successfully challenge them. In this context, intergenerational trauma inherent in migration can be treated not as a thing to inherit, nor as a thing to be passed down. In improvisation, we accept everything we bring inside of us, take in offers made by our performance partners and co-create a tableau that is the present moment.

SHOLTO BUCK AND STAYCI TAYLOR

Intergenerational Spaces and Trans-Tasman Places

Here, Sholto and Stayci get creative (queer-ative) with form, bending the essay to the will of their poetry and screenwriting practices, guided by the question: how can we recreate such notions of intergenerational queer space on the pages of an essay? Writing together in a digital document, Sholto and Stayci explore the interplay between writing for the screen, writing about the screen and collaborating on the screen. If, as Taylor et al (2023) argue, queer space is 'a space of potentiality where we can remake ourselves', then we contend the page can also facilitate such remaking and retaking of (queer) space. Buck's poems come from a series of poetic responses to the works of queer filmmakers, and Taylor's screenwriting practice disrupts screenplay conventions and point-of-view.

You are currently working on an erotic, philosophical cinema of heartache.

    TEOREMA, 1968
    (after Pier Paolo Pasolini)

    A winter scene: I lie in bliss. You stand
    over me, a shirt in the shape of a man.
    White briefs on the floor.
    This is an allegory told in clothes
    and the bodies that empty out of them.
    Cigarette ash falling on a bulge.
    Your spread wide tight
    cream pants and sadness in your eyes.
    I frame your luscious glance in perfect
    clean glass. A white glove on a hairy ass.

> Kiss the saint and then the star. No
> history could reflect this truth. What's real
> is fantasy. The memory of a thing
> that didn't happen. In the factory the bosses slacken.

In considering Narcissus's mirror, you have alighted on the screen as a pool for holding attention.

If, as YOU et al (2023) argue, queer space is 'a space of potentiality where we can remake ourselves', then?

```
                    YOU
    Each approach seeks to reconfigure surfaces, from the
     banal to the sublime, into atmospheric force fields.
```

Rich in imagery. Thorough in its quest for drama.

```
INT. NZ HOUSE OF REPRESENTATIVES — 8 MARCH 1985

Member of Parliament Fran Wilde presents a private
members' bill.

                    FRAN WILDE
          Behold the Homosexual Law Reform Bill.
```

Fran's wild!

> Gen(evieve) X was 17 the following year, when the bill went through.
> Gen(evieve) X was homophobic af.

You thread a personal narrative by kaleidoscoping into cinematic worlds, in turns erotic, violent, and contemplative.

Stories developed as a series of *beats*, recorded on *beat* sheets, sounds like a queer method already.

1993: You and your girlfriend in the badlands of (ha!) Northcote. Having been spied pashing in her little black van, you are trapped inside as it's rocked by thugs.

Performing as shifting subject positions, the speaker of your work finds humour, shelter and emotional truth in fantasy, even as reality collapses into his desires.

1993: Sitting with your girlfriend and a collective noun of muffdivers outside a Fitzroy café. Your girlfriend's friend Peach leers at the women passing by. You already know you're not comfortable with objectifying women in this way, let alone harassing them. You're wearing a floral dress gifted to you by a previous housemate whose vintage aesthetic you coveted (still do). You're at odds with the dress code. Peach points this out.

> As you type this, you keep being offered the peach emoji on the MacBook's toolbar, the international pictorial euphemism for appreciating ass.

Queer time, as argued by everyone's favourite trans-masc queer theorist, Jack Halberstam, might look like 'narrative without progress' (2011).

When you did your PhD, you developed an interest in Marcuse's theory of Narcissus as a figure who eluded normative labour structures, by carving out a distinct order of desire.

When you did your PhD, you channelled Jenny Schecter.

PhDs make fools of us all.

KNIFE + HEART, 2018
(after Yann Gonzalez)

In which I star as me:
the actress on the verge of tears.
Neck arched like a swan, lilting
synth or barn on fire. This is

my swelling password
protected aria, I'll tell anyone

you broke my heart.

In the nightness of my mood.
In the stare of a genital's eye.

I'm on a quest
for mystery. Chemical,
your slagging jaw
slow as a winding tape.

Switch / delete / death
into its perfect

theatre
a muscly thick

alchemy that spits
back what I know

I ran away
but even then

I woke up running.
Toward a telephone in an empty room.

Blue chandelier into red right angle
corridor. In the film,
you killed me.

Eye bored into parted lips.
Ornate,
my sailor outfit in the grass.

Kiss the mirror.
Jerk off slowly.

My belt, a sculpture of clasping hands.
This language is my only secret.

A slow arriving train and the fire of memory
burns into me like a negative. Here lies

my masterpiece: the long cinema
of obsession.

I was paradise's
burning son.

Fire fighting was an Olympic sport
and I starred as myself

in every crisis.

1990: In a side-room to the main event, Gen X lies prostrate with a broken leg at her own birthday party, while her boyfriend manages the tidy-up and exit strategy. She is, for some reason, surrounded by lit candles. Her friend, the lesbian, enters and tries to get some action. She is appalled.

'Screenness' here refers to surfaces that enthral your poem's speaker: a phone's diffuse glow; a wall through which muffled voices can be heard; the deep colour of analogue film.

```
INT. GRAD BALL UNIVERSITY OF OTAGO — 1989

YOU with someone else's parents, THE MUM and THE DAD.

The lesbian walks past.

                    THE DAD
              She looks like a man.

                      YOU
              She might as well be.

Despite the lesbian's transgressions, you hate yourself
for this.
```

You are interested in treating these surfaces as pools for generating metaphysical exploration.

1993: Drinking whisky you can't afford at a Southgate bar, you look out over the Yarra and tell your boyfriend of four years that you wouldn't rule out bisexuality. You're surprised by his resistance to this disclosure. You change the subject.

Your boyfriend cheats on you and you break up. His new girlfriend later accuses you of deliberately emasculating him by moving on to a female partner.

1996—ongoing:
Gen X phones the
IRD/ATO
bank
[insert service provider here]

posing as her girlfriend, because she's better at these calls.
A bonus of same-sex partnerships.

Your work moves through a series of ekphrastic responses to films and myths, interweaving them with personal experience and fragments of overheard, intentionally misinterpreted speech.

1976: Your mother enters the lounge, having put your three-year-old sister to bed. She joins you and your father watching celebrity chefs (and lovers) Hudson and Halls on television. They are camp and hilarious, uniting your young family in roars of laughter.

Halberstam celebrates the intergenerationality of queer spaces wherein folx 'do not "outgrow" certain forms of cultural activity' (2012); that is, the spaces and attendant antics where the decades between, say, Gen X and the Millennials are gaily disregarded.

INT. SPACES AND ATTENDANT ANTICS

GEN X and MILLY ENNIAL gaily disregard.

Gen X's father explains that it's not so much two men together that turns his stomach, but lesbians!

He is genuinely disgusted.

He is fearful.

There is something about the way he lets the word slide off his tongue.

As it were.

Images of multiple feminine slimy inner workings. Slugs.

Disgusting.

It will take Gen X a long time not to hate the word, even when she's ensconced in communities of lesbians and performing her own lesbian sex acts.

```
INT. MAKING AN EXHIBITION OF YOURSELF—DAY

Gen X waits in the wings, a helix of nerves and
excitement.

                        MC
            Introducing — the lesbian sex act!!
```

1995: The members of your lesbian share house give you a checked shirt for your 26th birthday.

SEBASTIANE, 1976
(after Derek Jarman and Paul Humfress)

I am writing in tribute
to the homoerotic theory
that died on those rocks
for love

I have cast myself in this poem
as Jarman's Sebastian, in order to give
credence to the notion
everything in this book happened to me

an arrow-pierced and bleeding
hawk with a spat out tooth, a saint
with the sky in my mouth

filigree green
delicate as nothing spider
I was never

so lonely as I was
when I was loved
by my oppressor

⋆

The men laugh
and bite each other's thighs
their pissing silhouettes
against the sky like gods
painting sun on muscle

I close my eyes
water drips from my beard, through my lips
my nipples, down my ass

I tense to depict
my suffering through movement
2-dimensional
a flat elegance

To be disgusted in the company of others
autocrat of myn own loneliness
a seagull crying in a storm

I reach my shell arm to the air
its tilting tiers, pearlescent
scintillans I can feel
resentment growing
at the edges of their joy

⋆

Morning wood
I throw swords in a pile
a lyre I
kneel to receive the pearl
plucked from sea
and wreathed upon the rocks

I fuck my foe on mythical
ground, wrestling
in the gush of waves
the sun bounces off
my armour and my red thong

I am dressed
for orgiastic combat

A pariah I
against my brethren for refusing
my commander's desires
am armed
with the cut stone of zeal

Sparkling droplets spiral
this violence feels theatrical

Cadmium thick
pig's blood painted on the sand

⋆

Salt ration, silver coin
cup of dice, idle
soldier fingering
the knife's edge

I whisper into
my jailer's open mouth

You don't need to go on
You don't need to rub that mineral scream

I unsheathe his boot
laurel crown
spat wine
I think about lips

Your laugh like an invisible hand
reaching down your mouth your hand
is tearing out your heart

From the love I didn't want
I know that I will die

lying with my mouth closed

⋆

It happens in slow-motion
coral ribbons run down

If I have regrets
like in the movies

my ass, perfect no matter what
curves against the sea

I take my breath
the archers take their place

You and your girlfriend redeem a fancy Wellington hotel package that was a gift.

On arrival, you are

INT. FANCY WELLINGTON HOTEL RECEPTION — 1998

hastily offered a twin room instead of the king suite ordered, and the receptionist is not taking no for an answer.

> RECEPTIONIST
> I'm not taking no for an answer.

The situation becomes quite hostile as you realise the woman is now insisting you take the twin because she can't fathom the alternative.

> RECEPTIONIST
> I can't fathom the alternative.

Later you settle for a drinks voucher by way of apology.

Your father was dying. Your partner arrived from Auckland and as they approached, your father announced

> DAD
> Now my whole family's here.

THEOREM, 1968
(after Pier Paolo Pasolini)

I am going to tailor my trousers and fuck
so many similar-looking men
to remember what it felt like
to kiss your hairy face. This is a futile quest
but what isn't. Concrete
platforms laid like a chess board.
I will make my life with what you left.
A footprint of a cloud on sand.
I will go where you might see me.
Standing around, the kind of thing
that happens every day. My love
killed me into a dream
and left me there. My silk tie
thrown down from a balcony.

Notes
1. Halberstam, Jack, *The Queer Art of Failure* (Duke University Press, 2011).
2. Halberstam, Jack, *Gaga Feminism: Sex, gender, and the end of normal* (Beacon Press, 2012).
3. Taylor, Stayci, Angie Black, Patrick Kelly and Kim Munro, 'Manifesto as method for a queer screen production practice', *Studies in Australasian Cinema* 17 (1–2), 2023, pp. 50–67.

JOHN KINSELLA AND ROBERT SULLIVAN

Vertical Dialogue

Verticality (JK)

1.
I still suffer every time I go down into the valley reserve and see the chimneys of the massive, ancient flooded gums destroyed during a so-called 'controlled burn' over a decade ago. Suffering is relative: to the trees themselves, to the many animals that made homes in their vast structures, and all the creatures that perished in that absurd burning. It is also relative to the biosphere and the creatures trying to persist in the valley in the here and now. But I do viscerally experience their loss: pins and needles, flushing, sleeplessness (on top of my sleeplessness) and nightmares when I do sleep. These were immense organic structures whose verticality promised spread and escape from regularity, whose every branch was anomalous to rise yet part of rise. For birds, height is security for roosting, feeding, and with the hollows of flooded gums, nesting. As 'feral' (and 'domestic') cats, foxes and humans move below, it's an alternative existence. Folded in the valley, height is tangent and shadow, it is a fracture in containment. I photograph the ones that survive to exclude their crowns out of respect for aspiration and alternate sense of height, breadth and correspondence to surroundings, and place the remnant chimneys firmly within the photo frame to show extent of loss. New stems from the root systems are hope, but they are still straggly and struggling after all these years. Other photographs show kangaroos negotiating the conditions: open pasture is feeding, loss of shade and soul of ecosystem is in crisis. Nothing is as simple as one species eating and feeding. And this is sacred Noongar Boodja where waterways form and connect with others whose formation is in yet other spaces, other language zones. Ballardong, Yued, Whadjuk. All of it was desecrated by the colonial surveying, fencing and then breaking into smaller farmlets and lots. It's ongoing, and the loss of these trees is a marker. My son Tim, also a poet, has written about the ancient flooded gum in town, outside a church, holding on. These

destroyed trees still have so much to say about spaces and verticality, the V of valley, flow, drainage, tangents, and widening into light.

2.
The limitations of aerials and phone towers are their radio frequency (RF) waves, the clearing of land to give them 'site', the shaving of hilltops to make them even higher. Verticality becomes erasure of verticality. In the breadth of their reach, they aspire down more than up. As drill core samples 'reveal' secrets underground and promise greater excavation, verticality towards the 'core' becomes exposure. As the well taps the artesian, the interior, the held, the 'reservoir' is brought vertically to air to be consumed. Well to tower, tangents to the core. Fractures in the biosphere.

3.
The verticality of launch: power and wealth, control and surveillance. To rise and curve then orbit. Parabolas and breaking out of the atmosphere. Everywhere, gravity ... overt and so subtle we drift endlessly. The contradictions of aspiration and exploration. The earthly desires of futurists, the fundamentalism of satellites. To send a message of love, to coax a war. And there I will be at the back door again this evening looking out for Venus, the evening star lifting the York gum even higher—not the tallest of trees, but tall enough, then taller. And if it's a cloudless night and it doesn't appear, I will direct ... supplication, evocation, invocation, entreaty? And it will be directed upwards ... or almost ... at least, above the false horizon of the valley ... the southern face which holds the sun later than here, where I view from, the chimneys of flooded gums already buried in shadows. And if the star doesn't rise, the 'wheatbelt frogs' (a recently declared species, as if knowledge can only ever be new and updated) will call it out, negotiating toxic residues from farm activities, forcing their top-of-head eyes into the sky-range of their 360 degrees, correlating satellites with spray nozzles.

4.
I have 'looked up' since I remember. I waited for something to appear out of the sky, from the stars. I saw a UFO and was interviewed by the Air Force. I wrote a book entitled *Visitants* about colonial invasiveness, which I understood was also about a fear of myself, ploughing in the 'wheatlands'.

Then I started looking down, losing the ability to find my way by the stars. My nights were always cloudy—smog closing in. Now I try to drive away the external light. Try to see deeper though my eyes are failing. I close my eyes, and each eye is a separate hemisphere, a different planetarium, and I wonder at what angle each sits to the other, what in fact can be vertical. All seems curved even when in heat I see icebergs float across my vision.

Verticality Too (RS)

Tāne Mahuta is our tupuna. He lies on Papatūānuku, the earthmother, with his legs in the air like the trees separating earth and sky. He is the god of forests, birds, every living being within the forest—the long-legged wētā, the noke, the giant and tiny snails, pekapeka bats, kōmako bellbirds, mokomoko lizards, moths and butterflies. The sun rises, the moon rises, in the canopy.

The noke or native worm is a vertical thing too—but unseen in its verticality. A snail has tentacled, vertical eyes. Trees and grass shake in the wind, and dust flies with pollen and sound.

So sound is vertical too. What do the ears of Papatūānuku hear? Are the ears of Tāne and Papa spirals hanging from vertical and horizontal beings?

When I think about trees I remember Vinod Raja's documentary about the Adivasi homelands, and their mined forests spiralling down into open cast pits. And I think of the paddocks running all the way across Otago and Canterbury with brief respites of mountains and remnant forests on private and public land. The saved forests are old—massive tōtara, trees and ferns jostling among waterways, caves and waterfalls. The climate is wet inside and around the forest. Beyond it is dry grass, and buildings.

But Tāne Mahuta is my tupuna. We are forest people us Ngāpuhi, and us Kāi Tahu. Our forests looked different. They had very old trees and very young trees and so many birds. Imagine the grub and insect life to feed such tall and small flocks.

*

I went up our mountain, Hikaroroa/Mt Watkin, in East Otago last year. We were guided up, but we took a wrong turn and ended up climbing over boulders and through taramea or 'Spaniard' grass—incredible needle-like leaves that cut my hands. I thought it was going to be a walk but really it was a climb. I fell a couple of times coming down. There were holes in between the boulders covered with ordinary long grass. An eighty-year-old kaumatua fell also on the way down the fenceline. Incredibly, he wasn't injured but he was sore. His leg had bent way back in the fall.

Yet at the top the view was high. We could see the flow of the Waikouaiti from the west as it moved to the lagoon at Karitāne. We could see the other members of the Āraiteuru crew, Pahatea and Kā Iwi a Weka. Aoraki or Mt Cook, to the norwest, was also aboard the waka which lies as a stone reef at Matakaea to the north.

Our whānau at Puketeraki paddle and sail waka here now. The whānau are building a new double-hulled waka. It'll be ready in a couple of months in time for spring. The wood is already showing polish. I watched the whānau sand with electric sanders. The gunnels haven't been placed on top of the hulls yet but the hulls are nearly finished. Then it's a matter of putting the crossbeams and boards between the hulls, and standing the poutokomanawa or mast up, making it stand tall in its wooden sleeve.

I've only sailed once on the lagoon, on Hauteruruku, after the dedication of our ancestral pā at Huriawa Peninsula as a site of national significance. Hei runga! And we'd raise our paddles. Hoe! And we'd dip into the sea. Ki uta ki tai.

Verticality Continuation (JK)

5.
I read Roberto Juarroz who doesn't, *yet does*, see trees like me. He hasn't named the type of tree (and I don't necessarily mean the straitjacket of 'species') and no doubt the tree he is thinking about reaches beyond the generic, closing me out of the place he associates with that tree, all its tensions and joys, and I cannot rise beyond the aphoristic, beyond its allusions. I cannot emulate and approximate a specific tree experience which means its symbols and lines and that's not enough responsibility to my way of processing. Interestingly, though English translation is on the facing page, and I don't speak Spanish, I go with the original 'Argentinian':

> El silencio cae de los árboles
> como frutos blancos,
> madurados bajo la piel de otra luz.[1]

because this reads vertically descending just as English to me—colonial language of aspiration and occupation—and light sticks out like a leaf bud or strip of bark twirling in a vigorous breeze. In other words, all the appendages and variations of verticals. Light, a key to the image if not the poem where silence dominates and 'erases' roads. Light, to me, is the most deceptive and splintering vertical of them all. But silence 'falls' from the vertical (the tree) and consumes all ('like' other things do in the poem, such as 'night' or 'snow'). The poem's talk of 'erasure' relies on accepting an illogical declaration or in accepting the absolute nature of the figurative. This moves away from the tree itself into analogy for human life and experience. In practical terms, *here* there is mainly silence around the loss of those flooded gums though one of the perpetrators did admit at the time, 'Yes, sadly lost a few of the old ones'. He then pointed out that if someone else had been in control it would have been 'worse'. I figure the catastrophe of all the houses, sheds, animals, trees of the entire valley burnt out. Smoke vertical enough to touch satellites, the evening star … no, more than that—consume them entirely.

6.
Habitation versus destruction in the exosphere. The long travels and travails of hydrogen, helium, nitrogen and oxygen molecules to reach each other. Here, a definition outside 'liminal' becomes necessary to reify presence. Satellites think they have the answer, in space and out of space. When I think verticality I end up here, without points of reference other than the earth I cannot quite reach. I am always looking down the vertical, questioning the stability of Jacob's Ladder. A residue of a system I left long ago. Stepping down into the stratosphere, micro-organisms. With the rubbish we deposit, eject and poison the upper atmosphere with, comes the microbes, the bacteria.[2] Some use the term 'thrive'. Vertical endgame thriving. People who pray to verticality might lose some of their prayers' energy there … mutating and transforming into new forms of liminality. Below, down here, the

pundits and profiteers, the leisurists and opportunists might call this a new frontier. Something to see through the portal on the way to the moon ... Mars. Definitions of speculative will shift, as they have before. Or speculative will become the tree chimney morphing into an ecosystem of numerous insects, birds, reptiles, marsupials, and I can name many of them as they were: moon moths, jewel beetles, galahs, ringneck-parrots, red-capped robins on lower limbs, brush-tailed possums, sun skinks etc. Etc, as adverb, is a grammatical quality of verticality ... and parsing.

Lucretius says, 'If it were not for this swerve, everything would fall downwards like raindrops through the abyss of space.'[3] All of this merges in the tree chimneys that look up out of the history of state-industry-driven 'controlled burns'. This is not the cultural burning, the cool burning of Noongar communities. This is not the gentle spread. It is the massive ejection of bush into atmosphere. It is vertical death. It is the creation of damaged and damaging space.

7.

You can measure the height of a tree with a clinometer. Or you can use the 'stick method'. Arm length, walk back, grip in the right position, 90 degrees, alignment, measure distance from tree to your footmark, and, hey presto, you have the height of the tree. In a forest this is not easy. A 'skill' my forester grandfather no doubt possessed. With the devastation of the valley, 'measurement' is all too easy. An induced spatiality predicated on measurement and the no longer measurable. An immeasurable consequence. To measure the retreating, over-taxed artesian water 'supply', deploy an acoustic probe. In the old open wells of a wheatbelt farm, walled with stone, the retreat was beyond measurability—only a saline crust remained. And when the water level rose, you measured the unpotable, cleared land glowing chemical all around. Trees on the edge of salt scald caught between life and death. And then you looked up at the constellations and marked yourself in time. To forget the gnamma holes of granite outcrops, to forget the origins of those constellations over this stolen, damaged country. Then to remember, unable to measure height, depth ... distance.

8.

Allusions to Verticality

When I was an addict
and often homeless,

I read some of Roberto
Juarroz's *Vertical Poetry*

translated by W.S. Merwin.
I lost my second-hand

copy long ago, or sold
it with other poetry books

so I could buy a drink
or score. I wrote poems

not in response
and then lost them.

I composed in memory
to forget. The saying,

'Head in the clouds'
was more than a joke

as I was frequently
falling or sinking

into the sea around
'Fremantle'. When

I make allusions
to verticality

it's merely political.
I have a system

for climbing onto the roof
without a ladder, and

for removing mud
from my shoes

during drought.
I fear contrails.

I agitate just as
the broken

washing machine
can't or won't. But

in my long sobriety
it's the breaking

of the meniscus
of exosphere: rockets,

decaying orbits
of satellites. I know

the location of each
and every meteorite

that's managed its
dark flight fall

to contest
verticality.

Verticality Too 2 (RS)

Poem for a Snail

You've seen me before chasing the pages
of Te Tiriti o Waitangi
But that was before, when I had an army of me
a willing retinue to flow out and grab
our sovereign treaties
But now I'm a snail on the run
trying to outpace the summer burn
the falling branches
trying to slide aside
from the landslides
and the million ponds
between me and the next meal
I could climb the atua trees
but they're falling
I could raise a tentacle
like a periscope
I could find a sturdy leaf
for a curly boat
but a pussycat or a possum
or a hedgehog would eat me
So I need to run
I am the largest snail here
it's my responsibility
to live on for diversity
This is my stump!

who gave the names here

Who gave the names here?

We know who made them
from our kōrero ō nehera

We know their parents
who stood between their parents

So I will fly in time
to see what is to be seen

Tāne Mahuta moving
over rocks, over valleys,
over trees, over leaves
and petals, moving over
inside earth, creatures, hanging
creatures, flying, climbing,
gripping, walking, crawling,
sliding and inching creatures,
twig, bark, leaf parts like
fingers, stumps, brachioles
as homes for huhu, for manu
for wētā, for ruru, branches
for snares, earth rustle litter
falls and felling of tāne
with his male side and his
female side

So who named it spaniard?
the perfumed oil of taramea
on our skin oil collected
drop by drop over home fires
despite its sharp leaves

So who named it parson bird?
or bell bird? Or wood pidgeon
or wax eye and why are the ones
that fly given English names
and the walking, wading, snuffling
birds left alone? Ha!

Notes
1. Roberto Juarroz, *Vertical Poetry: Recent poems*, ed and trans. Mary Crow (White Pine Press, 1992), p. 72.
2. www.science.org/content/article/microbes-survive-and-maybe-thrive-high-atmosphere
3. Lucretius, *On the Nature of the Universe*, trans. Ronald Latham (Penguin, 1970), p. 66.

The Landfall Review

Landfall Review Online

www.landfallreview.com

Reviews posted since April 2024
(reviewer's name in brackets)

April 2024
'A Bloody Difficult Subject': Ruth Ross, te Tiriti o Waitangi and the making of history by Bain Attwood (Sarah Christie)
The Call by Gavin Strawhan (Stephanie Johnson)
The Bones of the Story by Sandra Arnold (Michelle Elvy)
Light Keeping by Adrienne Jansen (Michelle Elvy)
Secrets of the Land by Kate Mahony (Michelle Elvy)
The Waters by Carl Nixon (Chris Else)
You Are My Sunshine and Other Stories by Octavia Cade (Tim Jones)
Little Doomsdays by Nic Low and Phil Dadson (Pat White)
Killer Rack by Sylvan Spring (Pat White)
A Long Road Trip Home by John Allison (Pat White)

May 2024
Spindrift: New & selected poems by Bob Orr (Tony Beyer)
Residual Gleam: Selected poems & translations by Roger Hickin (Tony Beyer)
Bushline: A memoir by Robbie Burton (Tim Saunders)
John Mulgan and the Greek Left by C.-Dimitris Gounelas and Ruth Parkin-Gounelas (Giovanni Tiso)
How to Disappear Completely by Nicholas Sheppard (Airini Beautrais)
Taken by Alex Stone (Nod Ghosh)
A New Eden: Betaverse Trilogy (Book 1) by Menilik Henry Dyer (Nod Ghosh)
Lioness by Emily Perkins (David Eggleton)

June 2024
Knowledge is a Blessing on Your Mind: Selected writings, 1980–2020 by Anne Salmond (Tom Brooking)
Blood and Dirt: Prison labour and the making of New Zealand by Jared Davidson (Robert McLean)
Do You Still Have Time for Chaos? by Lynn Davidson (Ash Davida Jane)
Blood Matters by Renée (Elizabeth Heritage)
Talia by Isla Huia (Siobhan Harvey)
Big Fat Brown Bitch by Tusiata Avia (Siobhan Harvey)
Transposium by Dani Yourukova (Siobhan Harvey)
Tung by Robyn Maree Pickens (Loveday Why)
Calamities! by Jane Arthur (Loveday Why)
a-wake-(e)nd by Audrey Brown-Pereira (Loveday Why)

July 2024
Ans Westra: A life in photography by Paul Moon (Max Oettli)
Te Awa o Kupu edited by Vaughan Rapatahana and Kiri Piahana-Wong (Gina Cole)
At the Point of Seeing by Megan Kitching (Tim Upperton)
A Game of Swans by Janet Wainscott (Tim Upperton)
In the Temple by Catherine Bagnall and L. Jane Sayle (Tim Upperton)
Night Shifts: Word from the heartland by Pat White (Denys Trussell)
Green Rain by Alastair Clarke (Denys Trussell)
Roof Leaf Flower Fruit by Bill Nelson (Denys Trussell)
The Unsettled: Small stories of colonisation by Richard Shaw (Rowan Light)
Articulations by Henrietta Bollinger (Francis Cooke)

August 2024
Selected Poems by Geoff Cochrane (Harry Ricketts)
Aucklanders by Murray Edmond (John Gibb)
Sandbank Sonnets: A Memoir by Murray Edmond (John Gibb)
Tell Me Gently by Ruth Arnison (Genevieve Scanlan)
When I Reach For Your Pulse by Rushi Vyas (Genevieve Scanlan)
A Liminal Gathering: Elixir & Star Grief Almanac 2023 edited by Iona Winter (Genevieve Scanlan)
Cranial Bunker by Stephen Oliver (Nicholas Reid)
Emergency Weather by Tim Jones (Gail Pittaway)
Detritus of Empire: feather/grass/rock by Robin Peace (Piet Nieuwland)
Stones & Kisses by Peter Rawnsley (Piet Nieuwland)
Some Bird by Gail Ingram (Piet Nieuwland)
100 Years of Darkness by Bill Direen (Piet Nieuwland)

September 2024
Dear Colin, Dear Ron: The selected letters of Colin McCahon and Ron O'Reilly by Peter Simpson (Ian Wedde)
Still Standing: A memoir by Anna Crighton (Sally Blundell)
Because All Fades by Freddie Gillies (Gill South)
The Mires by Tina Makereti (Rachel O'Connor)
Hoof by Kerrin P. Sharpe (Mary Macpherson)
PLASTIC by Stacey Teague (Mary Macpherson)
About Now by Richard Reeves (Mary Macpherson)
Neither by Liam Jacobsen (Vaughan Rapatahana)
Birdspeak by Arihia Latham (Vaughan Rapatahana)
Hopurangi/Songcatcher by Robert Sullivan (Vaughan Rapatahana)

Know How to Hold the Vā-Spaces

Robert Sullivan

Katūīvei: Contemporary Pasifika poetry from Aotearoa New Zealand edited by David Eggleton, Vaughan Rapatahana and Mere Taito (Massey University Press, 2024), 328pp, $39.99

This book is a pleasure to hold, and to dwell on. Hardbacks are rare these days, so to have a hardback edition is wonderful, and with a convenient placeholder ribbon as well. The dust jacket features *a gift of thanks* by Dagmar Vaikalafi Dyck and it reminds me of the Darcy Nicholas cover art in the Te Ao Mārama series, edited by Witi Ihimaera. The title, *Katūīvei*, is a hybrid term that means to navigate and to speak with two voices, like the tūī, which has two voice boxes, and conveys the reality of being Indigenous migrants to Aotearoa as peoples of the Moana. A few of the poets have Māori whakapapa, but most of the writers collected here come with intergenerational and recent migration narratives. Some choose to write directly about this, while others foreground a diverse range of other experiences in their poetics.

There is a brief introduction by the editors, and a history of Pasifika poetry by David Eggleton. The history could also have covered the influence of creative writing schools, such as the Manukau Institute of Technology's creative writing programme in Otara (2010–20), and given more information about the South Auckland Poets Collective (SAPC) as the lynchpin of poetry development southside. More could also have been said about Moana centres in other parts of Aotearoa, such as Wellington, Christchurch and Dunedin, but nevertheless this is a very welcome outline of the history of Pasifika poetry.

The tauhi vā, a Tongan term referring to the nurturing of relations, is pre-eminent and vital in these pages, but while the web of relationships encompasses the whole Moana, the scope of this anthology is limited to Aotearoa. There is acknowledgement of the predecessor anthologies *Mauri Ola* (Auckland University Press, 2010) and *Whetu Moana* (Auckland University Press, 2003), edited by Maualaivao Albert Wendt, Reina Whaitiri and myself.

The editors of *Katūīvei* also recognise *Lali* (1980) and *Nuanua* (1995), which were twentieth-century Indigenous Pacific anthologies edited by Albert Wendt. Another Indigenous anthology is *Indigenous Pacific Islander Eco-Literatures* (University of Hawai'i Press, 2022), edited by Kathy Jetñil-Kijiner, Leora Kava and Craig Santos Perez, which includes work by Māori and Pacific peoples throughout the region.

The effect of such anthologies is to elevate multiple Indigenous perspectives around wide-ranging sociopolitical, cultural, aesthetic and personal ideas and experiences. I'm also aware of the problematic term Indigenous, but I mean it here to represent the native peoples of the Pacific region who share difficult histories of colonialism.

This contemporary collection brings together the recent work of established poets including Maualaivao Albert Wendt, Tusiata Avia, David Eggleton, Karlo Mila and Selina Tusitala Marsh together with that of younger poets such as Courtney Sina Meredith, Amber Esau, Ria Masae and Nafanua Purcell Kersel. These are New Zealand-based writers, but the concept of vā is a reminder of other significant anglophone voices from the wider Moana region, such as the late Caroline Sinavaiana, Konai Helu Thaman, Craig Santos Perez, Brandy Nālani MacDougall, No'u Revilla and Wayne Kaumuali'i Westlake.

The exclusion of contemporary Māori voices—except for those Moana poets who whakapapa also to tangata whenua—is understandable, given the recent anthologies *Puna Wai Kōrero* (Auckland University Press, 2014) and *Te Awa o Kupu* (Penguin, 2023), which must be seen as part of this kōrero.

The number of poems from each poet was limited to three, which I felt could have been lifted in some cases in order to show the intergenerational growth and influences throughout the vā. It also demonstrates these authors' importance within the joined literature of Aotearoa and Te Moana Nui a Kiwa. But I am sure that the editors closely considered all of this, because there is a clear level of care shown in this anthology. As an example, the editors note that the opening poem by Marina Alefosio was performed during the government's formal apology to Pasifika communities for the dawn raids of the 1970s: 'We broke borders with broken accents to break the chains of fear ...'

Most of the poetry gathered here is lyrical, unrhymed, and meant for reflection. Some is clearly for oral performance, but also works wonderfully well for the page. A surprising number of new voices have emerged recently and are clearly flourishing. The poem by Rhegan Tu'akoi, 'Emails from Air NZ are the bane of my existence', unpacks corporate greenwashing. Onehou Strickland's 'Dusky Warrior' explores the personal impact of the white gaze: 'The Dusky maidens and warriors watch on from the stars now ...' the speaker in the poem sobs.

Nafanua Purcell Kersel uses the mundanity of electronic surveillance in her poem 'Face Recognition' to explore facelessness: 'The Placeholder Diversity Face/ The Sidekick Sista Face/ The brown face ...' Another emergent poet, Amber Esau, who describes herself as Sā-Māo-Rish, uses vocabulary and action from the video game 'Street Fighter' to describe the after-school activities of a group of teens:

> some cars reverse
> keep driving, creeps, keep driving
> they're honking big as a hadouken and quick
>   as one, too, quicker than
> the fingers we pull behind them. Keep driving,
>   creeps, we whisper 'til
> they leave, then shout.

Tim Gray's 'Homeless of the Heart' captures a perspective that isn't often heard from: someone suffering from clinical depression whose apartment in an expensive part of Auckland hides their condition: '... when everyone's/ gone for the day,/ I lie on my   back-soaked/ (circumstance-mattress),   pissed-stained-wetness ...'. Daisy Lavea-Timo, a former New Zealand poetry slam champion, in her values-centred poem, 'Fringe Dwellers', challenges Palagi misconceptions:

1. How did you get an A+?
2. You're here on the Pasifika quota, right?
3. Can't succeed in one world and can't succeed too much in the other
4. How much do you get an hour?

As if that dollar value = her worth

and then goes on to proudly affirm her fringe status: 'Organic-Superfood-Koko-Samoa bubbling in my stomach … Sitting in the margins and knowing how to hold the vā-spaces is a blessing …'

I highly recommend this anthology as a rich teaching and literary resource for high school and tertiary classrooms and libraries, and as a book for all New Zealanders. The relationships described here are not just beautiful, they feel vividly real and they're told with emotional truth.

Mana Vāhine
Emma Gattey

Gauguin and Polynesia by Nicholas Thomas (Head of Zeus Books, 2024), 453pp, $114

Australian anthropologist and writer Nicholas Thomas has long been drawn to 'intractable, complex, and hard to understand' characters, as he stated in a recent talk at Trinity College, Cambridge. For over four decades Thomas has been drawn equally to the Indigenous peoples, lands and culture of Oceania. His oeuvre insists on 'the capacity of Islanders, not least that of Islander women, to shape not only their own lives and their relationships with outsiders, but also the ways outsiders such as artists perceive and represent them.'

Enter Paul Gauguin, the 'artistic genius' tarred with the brush of 'colonial appropriation and sexual abuse' of young Polynesian women. In *Gauguin and Polynesia*, Thomas writes against 'received views' that amplify Gauguin's 'enigmatic symbolism' or his exploitative, colonialist character. Neither wholesale veneration nor cancellation of Gauguin is appropriate, Thomas argues, because both reactions erase Islander agency and mana.

Pitched as 'loosely biographical', his book circles between 'Gauguin' and 'Polynesia' as force fields interacting. And his retelling feels as original and potent as the infamous paintings themselves. *Gauguin and Polynesia* restores Polynesia to its proper place in the story; not as auxiliary to some Great/Bad Characters of History, but as evolving environment, society and culture, all of which enabled Gauguin's most powerful paintings (and, unexpectedly, ceramics).

Chronicling the extensive history of ambivalence around Gauguin, the book's primary achievement is to succeed, in Thomas's words, in 'rescuing the art from the artist'. Thomas recognises that 'Gauguin was at his most unreliable when he was talking about his own art.' He wrote to mislead, to boast. Moreover, this was an artist committed to aesthetic 'dissonance and arbitrariness', to deliberately opaque composition. Importantly, this book is not a character resuscitation. An inveterate narcissist who both subverted and succumbed to clichés, Gauguin is not, in the end, the main point. In revising the revisionist, Thomas aims not to vindicate the man himself, but to enlarge our understanding of the art and the conditions of its making.

This has important repercussions. If we remove Gauguin from the ongoing dialogue 'between Oceanic and European modes of expression', cancelling his artefacts, this is a different, more noxious form of cancel culture: it de-authenticates the subjects of his paintings and diminishes our knowledge of the many complex relationships within that cross-cultural dialogue. What Thomas has undertaken, with remarkable élan, is a salvage project— not of Gauguin but of his 'incoherent' body of work and what it can tell us (if we let it) about its Polynesian subjects and culture. It is a resounding, synaesthetic success. Thomas upends assumptions about modernity, civilisation, gender roles and relations, points to where these assumptions have misinformed our reading of particular artworks, and offers 'another way of seeing Gauguin'.

Shifting the landmarks of Gauguin literature, Thomas spins the globe. He begins with *te fenua* (te whenua/the land), suggesting that we cannot understand Gauguin's work without 'engaging more deeply with the environment, culture, history and people' of Polynesia, whose modernity has been both 'essential and invisible' to his oeuvre. Undertaking this analysis of Polynesia's impact on Gauguin, as well as its representation in his art, Thomas looks closely at each artwork and its context. He finds that the artworks themselves 'reveal a Tahiti that was both mythic and modern', adapting to colonialism while sustaining ancestral values and lifeways. The art speaks to place and identity, in ways that we cannot afford to ignore.

Structurally, Gauguin follows our introduction to *te fenua*. Working with a sparse documentary record, Thomas paints his human subject relationally. Gauguin is framed in relation to significant others, those who enabled his life's work: his mother, Aline Chazal; his guardian, Gustave Arosa; his beleaguered (and brilliant) wife, Mette Gad. Thomas pays attention to detail at the highest levels of historical abstraction (the dynamics of imperialism and colonialism, the core patterns of 'modernity', the nature of consciousness) as well as the most granular (when and where Gauguin contracted syphilis, his infelicity with the Tahitian language). He covers little-known crises in French colonial history, along with the unprecedented 'inter-island sovereignty' of the Pōmare dynasty; and he locates tīfaifai (the distinctive appliqué fabric that came to replace barkcloth in French Polynesia) and hiapo (the 'optically vibrant freehand painting' by Niuean women on fabric) within modern Oceanic art.

Meticulously, Thomas provides maps, a timeline, inflation-adjusted currency values, historical connotations of language, all to show that in the context of 'cross-cultural art and history' the reader must expect 'ambiguities of meaning and value to be inescapable'. The illustrations are stimulating, diverse, gorgeous. The matte reproductions of paintings, sculptures, daguerreotypes, lithographs, newspapers, tīfaifai and other objects of material culture—reproducing even the scored woodblocks of the *Noa Noa* prints—are of the highest quality.

We meet Gauguin in surprising roles: as stockbroker, mysterious aide in Spanish Republican plots, labourer on the Panama Canal, hit-and-miss ceramicist, sculptor and—yes—colonial opportunist. Obsessed with what he saw as the opulence of settler life in the French colonies, he was determined to 'enjoy the privileges of settler society', economic and sensual. But Nicholas Thomas, a skilful field anthropologist, is characteristically sensitive to local voice, knowledge and experience, and pays immersive attention to place and its formative powers. Moving back and forth between archipelagic and continental islands, his structural choices utterly 'entangle' the stories, showing the inextricability of Islander and 'French' art history in this context. Technically precise, multi-scaled and historically informed, *Gauguin and Polynesia* recalls the work of Greg Dening, Lana Lopesi and Kate Fullagar.

Beginning with the 'competent though not remarkable' art of Gauguin's Paris years (1874–79), we move to the 'radical' ceramic work and paintings produced in Brittany, then the decisive advances of the Martinique paintings, arriving finally at the Polynesian paintings. A gifted ekphrastic writer, Thomas conjures a gallery in the reader's mind so that we can witness 'Gauguin's vision of Polynesia emerging'. By subjecting each painting to the same close reading, the author bolsters the book's argument that the works 'do not all do the same things, or somehow advance a single or coherent project'.

Thomas perceives that Gauguin 'did a sort of justice to, and even rendered monumental, the lives of then-modern Polynesians'. One of the main things Gauguin's paintings can help us to see is mana wāhine: the agency, volition and decision-making of Indigenous women. A particular strength of Thomas's analysis is his empowering treatment of Gauguin's Tahitian 'wives', Teha'amana and Pau'ura, aged between 14 and 15 when they enter this narrative. He offers a compelling argument around *Mana'o tupapa'u* (*Spirit of the Dead Watching*) (1892), Gauguin's infamous voyeuristic nude of Teha'amana. In an admittedly 'eccentric' approach, Thomas reads the painting divorced from Gauguin's 'narcissistic' description. Paying close attention to the composition, mood and Polynesian textiles in the room, Thomas suggests a relational reading: though depicted as 'a prospective sexual partner and a nervous one', the prominent tīfaifai shows Teha'amana 'was also a person related to others, a bearer of a genealogy, linked with named places and marae, a maker and receiver of gifts'.

Thomas adds that uncritical reliance on Gauguin's account of the painting has sustained a 'pernicious' critique that diminishes Teha'amana's status by denying she had any traditional knowledge to pass on to him. Refusing to allow her to remain collateral damage in culture wars, Thomas undoes this erasure and denial of her mana, noting that his own experience in the Pacific contradicts the assumption that younger generations are 'so disconnected from their culture as to have "no relation" to it'.

Moving along, Thomas analyses *Teha'amana* (1893), which shows the titular subject dressed, decorated and posing herself 'in a fashion that accentuates her presence and dignity'. Painted one year after *Mana'o tupapa'u*, this work 'reverses the implications of ... power and disempowerment that are inescapable in the notorious nude'. Here, Teha'amana is 'a woman of status with a formidable genealogy'. Thomas argues that even when 'clumsily' expressed, Gauguin's paintings of Islanders are 'a response to the commanding personality of an individual'; an acknowledgement of the sitter's sovereignty or mana; a concession that Tahiti was 'a place still shaped by Polynesians'; and absolutely representations of 'the individuality and dignity each [sitter] possesses'.

Contrary to Gauguin's 'discursive red herrings' or explanations, *Nevermore* (1897) is a portrait of maternal grief: it depicts no simple nude but the loss of Gauguin and Pau'ura's newborn son. Thus, muting Gauguin's voice and dialling up the historical and biographical context, Thomas turns our vision to Pau'ura, training our eye to see beyond the propaganda. Through this pointed emphasis on Islander women's agency, resistance and socio-political power, we are encouraged to look at Gauguin's Polynesian paintings to see not only loss through colonisation, but also agentic response, dynamism and inalienable mana.[1]

Critical and compassionate, Thomas helps us to see better. These portraits have been encrusted with Gauguin's polemic, his sexual powerplay and Big-Man-of-Art posturing. What we fail to see, when we denounce Gauguin as simple predator, is the women themselves: their desires, choices and self-representation. By bestowing 'presence and a calm ... power upon the person represented', Gauguin's portraits of Polynesian women 'acknowledge[d] the power that the person actually has'.

A core part of Thomas's thesis is the innate unknowability of two things: first, any 'objective' meanings of the paintings themselves; and second, what Gauguin intended to achieve through these representations. Rather than focusing on the artist's immorality (in current or historical terms), Thomas argues that the primary issue is the 'sheer eclecticism' and ambiguity of Gauguin's work.

In his book *The Return of Curiosity* (2016) Thomas noted that all museum artefacts bear 'a particular uncertainty: it is both what it was and what it is'.[2] Artworks bear the same ambiguity or multiplicity, which gives rise to the 'paradox of physical immediacy and nebulous identity'. In other words, we may stand in front of a painting, intimately confronting its aesthetic power, but remain unable to grasp any clear meaning. This 'significant ambiguity' means that controversial paintings—like ethnographic artefacts—are opportunities for individual and collective reflection, learning and dialogue.

While Gauguin's incorporation of Oceanic artforms into his paintings is now commonly viewed as 'reprehensible, as cultural colonization', Thomas argues that this 'gambit' was 'inherently contradictory'. Echoing his apologia for museums, he argues that '[i]f Gauguin took something from local tradition to use as suited his purpose', through the very use of those motifs, his artworks 'affirmed … that the Tahitian landscape was powerfully and permanently defined by Polynesian spirituality'.

Thomas takes us beyond ideology, binaries and simple, easy-to-peddle narratives (occasionally known as cancel culture). In doing so, he reminds readers what we risk losing, what we fail to see, in subscribing to any of the above. *Gauguin and Polynesia* reminds us that we have more options. Thomas deliberately issues no verdict on condemnation or rehabilitation. There is no judgement here, only fascinated agnosticism: Thomas explaining why it is 'impossible to reach any settled conclusion about what Gauguin did, who he was, and how finally his work should be valued'. We cannot simply *end* these conversations: we go on revising and revisiting conclusions and interpretations.

A cynical reader might wonder whether Thomas is trying, like the major museums that vex him, 'to have it both ways'. Given the magnetism of a Gauguin blockbuster exhibition, such museums play it safe, 'vaunting the art, while inviting debate'. But this book is a firecracker. It does not meekly welcome debate but throws down gauntlet after gauntlet, accepting and reissuing the challenge to show why history and art *matter*.

The fruit of 40 years of frustration, fascination, scholarship and dialogue in Oceania, *Gauguin and Polynesia* is a relentlessly good read. Thomas points to what cannot—ever—be known. And what questions, therefore, are worth asking. (Even if a painting 'will never be definitively explained', what can we learn through wondering?) Through careful critical reading, Thomas injects nuance, colour and entropic life into these entwined histories. Destabilising the orthodox line on Gauguin, he advocates instead for new ways of seeing.

Notes

1. See also Nicholas Thomas, *Islanders: The Pacific in the Age of Empire* (Yale University Press, 2010).
2. Nicholas Thomas, *The Return of Curiosity: What museums are good for in the twenty-first century* (Reaktion Books, 2016), pp. 50, 51, 53.

The Face of the Deep
David Herkt

Marlow's Dream: Joseph Conrad in Antipodean ports by Martin Edmond (Index Press, 2024), 252pp, $45

Deliberately occupying the shifting shoals between the tides of history and dream, biography and literary commentary, autobiography and fiction, Martin Edmond's boundary-challenging *Marlow's Dream: Joseph Conrad in Antipodean ports* is a singular book. Few writers from Australasia possess Edmond's range. His biographical subjects include the New Zealand painters Colin McCahon and Philip Clairmont, as well as *The Expatriates*, a revealing account of four New Zealanders making their reputations in Britain. There is the autobiographical *Bus Stops on the Moon*, an exploration of his time working with the Red Mole theatrical group, 1974–80, and the more intellectually peripatetic *Chronicle of the Unsung*, where periods in Edmond's personal history are shuffled with moments in the lives of Sir George Grey, Rimbaud and van Gogh.

Edmond's gaze is invariably slantwise, and deeply researched. He weaves his knowledge into knots and nets, seldom in an expected or pre-ordained manner. He is never a disembodied, or disengaged observer. The boundaries of invention and fact in his work are hazy, just as they are in life; he is a storyteller, intimate and enlightening. His voice is frank, but there are no sureties.

With this in mind, Joseph Conrad (1857–1924), merchant-mariner and writer, is perhaps Edmond's ideal subject. Their psychic worlds overlap. Both are preoccupied with the blurring boundaries of the self and human enterprise on the edges of empire: Africa, South America, and the archipelagos north of Australia—or even further out, upon the boundless 'sea-roads' themselves.

Both writers also have their personal origins far from the centre. While Edmond was born in Raetahi near Ohakune, in the volcanic centre of New Zealand's North Island, Joseph Conrad (originally Józef Teodor Konrad Korzeniowski) was the son of cultured Polish minor aristocracy with revolutionary political beliefs for which the family faced official sanctions. He was a bookish, somewhat sickly boy who would become a seaman, firstly on French ships, then under the 'Red Ensign' in the British merchant marine. As well as Polish and French, Conrad became a fluent speaker of English and it was in that language that he wrote his first novel, *Almayer's Folly*.

Edmond devotes some space to the crucial moment on Conrad's second-to-last voyage when his vocation as a writer was recognised by another. Amid the many spectral presences that hover both in and around Conrad's work, it was William Henry Jacques, a Cambridge graduate with tuberculosis, who was the prime mover. He was a passenger on the *Torrens* when the 36-year-old Conrad was serving as the ship's first mate. The pair struck up a convivial acquaintance based upon a mutual fondness for literature.

On a stormy evening at sea at the end of a discussion devoted to Gibbon's *History*, Conrad suddenly asked, 'Would it bore you very much in reading a MS in a handwriting like mine?' Jacques assented and received a fold of papers. The next day he returned the manuscript of the as-yet incomplete *Almayer's Folly* to Conrad.

'Is it worth finishing?' the author asked.

'Distinctly,' Jacques replied.

'Were you interested?' Conrad inquired further.

'Very much,' was the answer.

A silence fell, rolled upon the billows of the sea. 'Is the story quite clear to you as it stands?' Conrad continued to press.

'Yes, perfectly,' came the reply.

This was the extent of the brief exchange which, in effect, would change one man's life, English literary history, and to some degree contemporary Western culture—from movies to music. Edmond's account of the encounter includes one of the longest quotations from Conrad in *Marlow's Dream*—and centralises the meeting to his life and career.

Earlier in the book, Edmond had remarked upon the fact that, while a seaman, Conrad had used the pages of an English Bible, printed on rice-paper, to roll his cigarettes, reading as he went. The cadences of the King James Version echo through Conrad's narration of this fortuitous meeting with Jacques. The encounter was a revelation, a visitation, and an affirmation of vocation.

Jacques himself would die soon after the voyage. With the eventual submission of *Almayer's Folly* to T. Fisher Unwin in 1895 and its acceptance, Conrad began the publication of the series of books and short stories that made his reputation.

Edmond frequently situates himself as both observer and the observed. *Marlow's Dream* begins with an amble through his own life—a mishmash of 1970s King's Cross, forgotten nightclubs like the Manzil Room, and the warrens of long-gone second-hand bookstores in the Sydney of that era. In one bookstore he purchased two books by Conrad: *Almayer's Folly* and *Tales of Unrest*.

His method has always been that of the involved participant, of the flâneur, and the psychogeographer. Similar writers spring to mind, from Iain Sinclair with his 'orbital' walk of London, to Walter Benjamin, with his observations of Moscow and Paris, to Baudelaire and Poe. The stance of a wandering observer of urban life as a perspective in fact goes further back. The Venetian traveller Marco Polo and the Arabian historian Ibn Khaldun also come to mind.

But additionally, Edmond travels deeply into the psyche. In a book containing many portents and messages from beyond, he has an 'encounter' with Conrad in a dream and this first intimation leads his readers into a world whose extent will be later explored. 'The details of my life are gathered like shards of a great mirror in which destiny will be revealed,' the dream figure of Conrad explains to Edmond, lighting a cigar. 'It is not so. Nothing will be revealed.'

'We return to every place we've ever been,' he continues. 'Oceans of paper voyaging on. It is necessary to invoke eternity.' Much in the way of the infinite metaphysics of Borges, the mazy paths of G.K. Chesterton's short stories, or the labyrinths of London in the works of the opium-addicted Thomas De Quincey, Edmond layers the mystery of forking routes and shadow-lines over his text, placing the artifice of latitude and longitude upon the face of the deep, in a voyage led by phantoms.

More prosaically, the essence of *Marlow's Dream* is this 'return' to places—a recounting of Conrad's journeys in the merchant ships the *Duke of Sutherland*, the *Loch Etive*, the *Otago* and the *Torrens*, and the ports in which they docked in the Antipodes. On the *Duke of Sutherland*, taking general cargo out and wool on return, Conrad made his first voyage to Australia. The ship spent more than five months in Sydney because of difficulties gathering goods for the trip back to England. It would be a lengthy stay for Conrad, during which he gained a full and expansive acquaintance with the Rocks area of the city and its characters.

During his voyage in the *Loch Etive* he heard stories that would be transmuted in his later work. There was the steamer *Jeddah*, whose 21 crew abandoned the crippled ship to its fate during a storm, with over 800 Mecca-bound pilgrims on board, only to later discover the ship and its passengers had survived. This incident would become part of the plot of *Lord Jim*. There was also the story of an officer who killed a man and escaped onto another ship that would be the basis of Conrad's short story 'The Secret Sharer' and would also be used in the novel *The Shadow Line*.

During the return to Europe, Conrad assisted in the rescue of men from a sinking brig in the Atlantic near the equator. The brig's end came quickly. 'Far away, where the brig had been, an angry white stain undulating on the surface of steely-grey waters, shot with gleams of green, diminished swiftly without a hiss …' Conrad wrote, and 'the great stillness after this initiation into the sea's implacable hate seemed full of dread thoughts and shadows of disaster.' This was the moment, Edmond explains, when Conrad 'came to understand the otherness of the sea, its indifference to men and to ships'.

Conrad then commanded the *Otago*. At port in Mauritius, he became involved with two women. One was the teenage daughter of a ship's chandler or stevedore, the other a respectable French woman in her early twenties. Both eluded him, though the echoes of the first might remain in Alice Jacobus, the young woman who languorously reclines in her rose garden in a short story 'The Smile of Fortune', with its eerie and voluptuous sensuality.

He pursued the second, Eugénie Renouf, romantically. There were meals with her family, parlour games, visits to Conrad's ship and to the botanical gardens, only to discover upon his proposing marriage that she was engaged to another man. Conrad did not take the rejection well and in a final communication, as Edmond recounts, 'said that he would be thinking of the fortunate couple on their wedding day—

and that he would never again return to Mauritius. He never did.'

In the penultimate section of *Marlow's Dream*, titled 'Phosphorescence', Edmond explores three of Conrad's short stories of the so-called 'Otago Cycle' in greater depth: 'Falk', 'The Secret Sharer' and 'A Smile of Fortune', adding in 'The Planter of Malata' and 'Because of the Dollars'. He teases out these works and their links to Conrad's life. It is an exemplary piece of involved literary criticism where the stance of the commentator-reader, the subject-author and the writing are not abstractions but are intertwined human involvements. Consequently, this portion of Conrad's oeuvre is seen from new angles, in new lights. It is a mass of connections, resembling to some degree those *aides-memoires* or 'maps' created by the great Polynesian navigators, constructed from sticks, shells and knots of string, with arcs of reed to represent tidal currents.

In the book's final section, titled 'Marlow's Dream', Edmond examines Conrad in terms of the book his reader has just encountered: as history, biography, autobiography, dream, allegory, mystery and fable. Conrad's narrative devices—the various interlocking witnesses, the character of 'Marlow' who relates many of Conrad's stories, and indeed the first-person narrator himself—become a meditation on storytelling. This self-referential twist and the boxes-within-boxes of Conrad's plotting frequently form the basis of Edmond's analysis, as does his own personal involvement.

Marlow's Dream is rich; however, it does not fit contemporary categories neatly and may not gain the audience it deserves for that very reason. It is a vagrant volume, in the best possible sense of the word, embodying its great subject, observing and extending it, while adding information and an analysis of the consequences. Further observations of other of Conrad's Southeast Asian works—*Victory*, for example, and the novels of the so-called 'Lingard Trilogy'—may have aided the thesis.

Edmond's exploration takes its reader into the mysteries of creation, of human life, of colonial history, speculations of infinity, and eventually to the very edge of the known world. Written by an author who is prepared to take risks, *Marlow's Dream* is a fitting memorial to Joseph Conrad's legacy.

Dark Calls It a Day
Michael Hulse

Still Is by Vincent O'Sullivan (Te Herenga Waka University Press, 2024), 122pp, $30

'Been a lovely day, hasn't it?' someone might say, and you might reply: 'Still is.' How very like Vincent O'Sullivan, to title this collection with words that come from everyday usage but can carry a potent charge, quietly insisting on the continuum of existence. 'A day goes near perfect as morning makes it,' a poem here begins; and it ends, watching the sea,

> Our minds for once unbothered
> at being minds. Tides haul swathes of light,
> late, westing. Dark calls it a day.

Nothing here is difficult, but still the words are dense with complex thought and emotion. The stressed syllables in that second sentence are nicely paced across line-break and punctuation, but the sense of richness owes only a part of its fullness to veteran skills. Overwhelmingly, this is a self, enjoying the simplicity of being, the pleasures of seeing, and the acceptance that darkness will come and that that is okay.

Dark has called it a day for Vincent, and his family, friends and readers are left with memories and words. At the other end of the world, I sat at 2.30 in the morning at this laptop and tuned to his requiem mass in Wellington, expecting to be in tears. And so I was. But soon they were tears of laughter, thanks to the deadpan grace of those who knew and loved Vincent best. How brilliant New Zealanders are, I thought, and how true to his spirit is this pitch-perfect mischief amid the grieving.

It was at a poetry festival in Toronto that I first met Vincent, in April 1991. The dry wit of his reading sent me to buy *The Butcher Papers* and *The Pilate Tapes* at the bookstall, and I warmed to him immensely in conversation. He for his part liked my poems and my interest in Allen Curnow, and busied himself back home setting up a reading tour of New Zealand for me, with British Council help. The flight from Auckland to Wellington rocked in crosswinds as it approached over Cook Strait, and I told Vincent at the airport that I still felt unsteady on my feet, only to have him answer, 'That'll be 'cause we're having an earthquake.' Said, of course, in the flattest of tones, as though it were the most usual thing in the world. The friendship that grew from these beginnings was renewed at intervals in England and Germany, and my respect for his poetry, fiction and plays, as well as his work as biographer and editor, has steadily deepened over the years.

'Poetry's half the story,' he writes in *Still Is*. 'What it misses, that's the other.' Thinking of his writing outside poetry might be the way to recover that other half, but the truth is that all of his writing was poetry by other means. *Shuriken* is a play about the impossibility of the Japanese and New Zealanders understanding each other at the first POW camp for Japanese in the world, but it's also about the sheer poetry of everyday (male) speech. His novel *Let the*

River Stand has the same common-speech brightness of invention on every page. 'Mum'll have mine for yo-yos if I'm this late again.' 'If she was any thicker, Bet said, the timber mill would have started logging her.' The language of all his writing is built on foundations in the poetic colour and wit of ordinary talk.

On top of that is the sense of structure acquired by an indomitable intellect. That intellect started out with the underpinning of Irish Catholicism (only one generation separated him from the ancestral country) and was contoured by informed familiarity with the arts, philosophy and politics, and more. In his earlier poetry, conceptual architecture mattered to him, and the Butcher and Pilate sequences, as well as *Brother Jonathan, Brother Kafka*, are the superb results. From the 1990s this controlling, forming component became less apparent in his poetry and he preferred to write in a loose *parlando*, often as if talking to himself. One poem in *Still Is* consists of four long-lined quatrains (even rhyming *abab*) and reads like a refugee from *Brother Jonathan, Brother Kafka*; the poems around it are all in the relaxed thinking-aloud manner of the late poems. The key structure that survived to the end, despite (or because of) his undeceived knowledge of the world's ways, was Christianity:

> Nietzsche's horse. The nag he hugged to madness
> in Torino, its veins churning his ears.
> The world is thrashed, or does not exist.
> The appalling pointlessness of Christless tears.

That is the whole of a brief piece in *Still Is*. Vincent was never more fully the child of the faith he was raised in than in those last six words.

His undeceived knowledge is everywhere, often voiced explicitly in asides. In *Let the River Stand*, at one point in a conversation between Alex and his aunt her words are glossed as 'said not with irritation so much as an amused acceptance. And underneath the amusement, weariness. As if her nephew had remarked that boys kill flies, men go to war, women are always disappointed, one way or another.' So much fundamental (from her perspective: bleeding obvious) knowledge is stored in this aunt, and her weariness with it all is overlayered with amusement and acceptance; and all of this has first to be in the author before, matryoshka-like, he can contain within himself this imagined woman.

The poems of the last 20 years seem almost invariably to have more to them than meets the eye, nine-tenths of their meaning below the surface and only the tip visible. This is more than a mature style; it is a late style, a style that pushes beyond the complexities to relish simplicities, as death comes closer. In fact their secret really is often that there is no secret at all: Vincent in old age could be contented watching bees, birds, the tides and the light. There is no reason why this shouldn't be valued as wisdom; it's a lot better than raging against the dying of the light. In 2004 the final poem in *Nice Morning for It, Adam* cued us to the dominant note of the late poems:

... 'Still at your window,' they say, 'can't you give it a rest?' Not on your life, tell them, not on your earthly.

And so, in *Still Is* we have 'First Wing', in which a kōtare is seen when he's barely awake. The voice of his knowledge contributes 'halcyon' and 'kingfisher' before he turns his back on the mythological world the words open:

> The halcyon frozen again to myth.
> Kōtare we say, back to words we're
> at ease with. Brilliance snapped from bright.

These moments are sufficient, and Vincent time and again simply notes them in a celebratory spirit, happy to accept each day. We know of course how productive he remained in his last years, so this isn't an image of a beatifically indolent sage; rather, as with Czeslaw Milosz, we are witnessing a commanding mind understanding that celebration is the defining achievement of the spirit in its twilight years.

All very well. But there is another poem, also with a bird at its heart, that strikes a different heart-breaking note. This is all of 'Sunday Night, Port Chalmers':

> Willie Nelson singing, 'Why not take all of me.'
> Eleven p.m., almost. A southerly predicted.
> I'll wake about three, if I'm lucky,
> to hear the cold front battering in,
> flaring the wall a few inches from where
> I lie, hearing the constant drive
> of one thing towards another: as earlier
> this week, one o'clock church bells ringing,
> and an old man at home with a small green
>   bell
> as though ringing for tea, because an
>   albatross,
> the first of the royal albatrosses, has majestied
> in at the Heads for the breeding season:
> one, so we're told, who may have ridden
> and skimmed the oceans twelve months
> without touching down. Bells have rung for
>   so much
> less. Riding the calm and the storm and the
>   gift
> of high persistence, like weather itself, to
>   survive.
> I hope I wake at three to hear life barrelling
>   in.

He knows that the three unassuming words 'if I'm lucky' may be taken two ways here—if I'm lucky enough to get four hours' sleep (the sleeping rhythm of the old being what it is), or: if I'm lucky enough to wake at all. That strikes the keynote of the piece. This wonderful (and wonderfully simple) poem about the closeness of death presents the self in the largest of contexts, among the formidable movements of wind and weather and migrating birds and survival, and its closing line, like the words 'if I'm lucky', remains perfectly capable of being read in two ways, except that now the balance has been adjusted—introducing the words 'hope' and 'life' lends a deeply moving dimension to that final sentence.

'I am surprised how one comes to seem someone else, the minute one begins to write,' Emily observes in her notebook in *Let the River Stand*. Vincent's endeavour in his late poetry was always to overcome that sense of seeming someone else, and to write from the heart of the self, and in 'Sunday Night, Port Chalmers' he does just that, in the most unassuming and tranquil of ways. It's worth saying that this is the sense of self of a very modest man. In my experience, it was virtually impossible to get Vincent to say a single word about his own writing, which must make him unique in the history of poetry. When he wrote from under the shadow of death, he did so as if his own life weighed no more in the balance than that of the starling, say, in 'How Things Are'. This takes some doing.

Two other thoughts arise from 'Sunday Night, Port Chalmers'. One concerns the discreet way he plays with the word 'royal' before observing a little later, 'Bells have rung for so much/ less.' I recall my English grandmother telling me her childhood memory of bells ringing to mark the relief of Mafeking, and I rather suspect Vincent's thought is of those occasions when church bells across the British Empire rang for royal weddings and births, for military victories, and so on. It would be very much in harmony with his old-age feelings about the natural world (as well as with his Irish roots) if he were contrasting the ringing of bells on such occasions with the achievement of the albatross, which (he plainly feels) truly merits the ringing of bells.

The other footnote concerns Vincent's increasing scepticism in later life about anthropocentric views of the world. One poem in *Still Is*, nicely titled 'To Accept Being Human', shows that he could still be waspish, for all the serenity:

> I give thanks we were cradled in branches,
> that we moved on so surely to hands daubed
>   in caves.
> I give thanks to the dragged knuckles
> and the penetrating gaze. I'd be so proud
> were Silverback an ancestral name.
> I watch viewers at the rail of the ape
>   enclosure.
> I'm at one with ordure accurately flung.

Ha! We're going to miss him.

Let the Birds Sing
Elizabeth Smither

Bird Child & Other Stories by Patricia Grace (Penguin, 2024), 272pp, $37

In 2004 Patricia Grace and I flew to Spain to attend the 6th International Conference of the Short Story in English at the University of Alcalá, the theme of which was 'Crossing Boundaries'. In the picturesque town where Cervantes was born we marvelled at splendiferous academic robes, and we stood reverently in the doorway of the room where doctorate students argued their theses while an adversary, named the devil's advocate, challenged them from an alcove.

Patricia and I faced nothing so formidable: we read our short stories to small but attentive audiences; we attended papers on familiar and esoteric subjects; we went to a banquet where most of the seven courses were meat; and we were escorted to collect our fees by a student minder.

Listening to Patricia read, I was struck by her poise. When I had looked across the aisle during the flight she was sleeping with her hands lightly clasped in her lap. Her stories have this poise, though they are handed over to a variety of myths concerning adults, children, fish and birds. Each part is fully formed, whether it is about the moon, the prescription for evading an enemy, a bird ostracised like a human, a pile-up of bossy-boots aunties, someone sulking at the bottom of a grave, a disillusioned departmental adviser, or a miss-singing tūī.

The language is clear sighted, often brilliant, full of laughter: 'a middle slice of bacon and egg pie' (which took three cafés and two days to find) … 'arms heavy as tyres' … 'the sky was pale, stretched, pulled like balloon rubber to a white horizon' … 'ankles flopping over the tops of her shoes like sponge cakes overflowing their baking tins' … 'Got me a monkey to look after' (Uncle Kepa makes good his promise: not a monkey but a real boy) … 'Children had been instructed to visit God in the church once a day so they would become holy' (instead, they get the giggles) … 'At their feet were white laceworks of smashed sea'.

In 'Bird Child', the story that anchors the collection, the irresistible moment of birth coincides with the moment of must-be-resisted death at the hands of stalking enemies. The child's first indrawn breath must be stoppered, resulting in the child's death. The spirit of the child enters into a bird named Kaa. With infinite care, removing the minutest traces of their passage from leaves and forest floor, they reach a river and prepare to cross. Despite the danger their preparations are orderly and carried out without panic; everyone has a function.

The cause of this, Puawhaanganga, has behaved like an artist, seeking out a log of wood he has seen in a dream, intent on carving a new and superior taiaha. Like Henry Moore, he intends to release the form within. A fantail disturbs him and his own sense of solitude. It is in this dereliction that the slaughter of his people occurs: 'He ran through the forest to the clearing where he witnessed the smouldering remains of homes and storehouses, the heads of his wife and his esteemed sister spiked on poles.'

'Sun's Marbles' offers light relief, laced with humour: 'When Māui booby-trapped Sun, then clobbered him over the head with a hunk of bone shaped like two parts of a bootmaker's last, he won, for all time, high praise as the pioneer of daylight saving.'

And lists must be mentioned and birdsong translated: *creak* and *croak*, *tittle* and *rattle*, *sing song*, *ding dong*, *ki runga*, *ki raro*, *bubble* and *squeak*, *tihei*, *dur*, *whiti whitia*, *gargle-argle*, *tāiki ē*, *tiramarama*, *tīkiti* ('The Parson Who Thought She or He Was a Bishop'). And in 'Bird Child', there's this:

> Red is dawn-sky
> Red is underwing
> Red is evening
> You are adorned
> In the sacred colour,
> Fly …

'Nature Is the Source of Everything as it Is' reminded me of Douanier Rousseau's painting *The Dream*, with its lush greenery and the nude like an add-on. The philosophy to which the stories tend is: 'finding a balanced recipe'. Otherwise it might be 'Holy crap!' Hope is less effective than kindness, than the gathering of others, summoning resources. 'Sorry don't wash with me. Shut up about sorry. Put your clothes on. Get home, get in the shower.' ('Green Dress').

Uncle Kepa has 'plate hands' large and thick to enclose and comfort, to bang together as if raising dust, and this is where Patricia Grace stands. Two children might hollow out a loaf of fresh bread on the way home but the crust's nest remains.

There is a space in the stories that is waiting to be filled: dialogue turns into a quarrel; a disillusioned civil servant pats a dog and enters a conversation; a wet child turns up on the doorstep; a marine offers three packets of chewing gum; green is chosen for a wedding dress; a child has her forehead cut by a piece glass. There are descriptive passages that resemble a scientific experiment, where steps are carefully enumerated:

> In the early morning [Merana] had taken Lizzie out up to her neck in the sea and stayed with her until the tide went down. All that happened was that Lizzie had whitened and went soft, and the boils that had been red and plummy became motley and pale like birds' eggs. ('Boils')

Aunty Sandra, Aunty Zelda, Aunty Lola are close cousins of the Dublin knitting women Ann Patchett describes in her essay 'How Knitting Saved My Life Twice':

> When I dropped a stitch I simply walked up to any female person who was older than I was and handed her my knitting. If there was a woman in Ireland in the summer of 1983 who didn't know her way around a dropped stitch, I never met her.[1]

Child-rearing is a work in progress: 'They were indulgent parents inclined to put unacceptable behaviour down to teething problems, hyperactivity, high intelligence or precocity.' Merana's father in 'Departure' is a prototype of the good father: loving, self-sacrificing.

> He rolls about on his chair, laughing, wiping tears from his eyes over a silly photograph of his wife's feet when he goes off to war. On the wharf Mereana mistakes the troop ship for a huge building until it starts to move.

'Girls make me happy,' Watson says to his wife, Annie, in 'Matariki All-Stars'. There are seven daughters, and when Annie dies his worries begin: periods, boobs, buying a bra. When one of his girls is kidnapped by his sister he gets her back. He gives up his job, paints the house, saves enough to buy his girls new clothes.

> They turned to face him and began jumping about and clapping, like Americans on sitcoms, so excited he felt sorry for them.
>
> 'From the shop?'
> 'Awesome, Dad.'
> 'Aunty Zelda will help you,' he said.
> That stopped them.
> 'Nah. Nah, Dad.'

Material goods may be in short supply but there are aprons made from blackout material when the curtains are taken down; there are marigold petals and leaves to decorate a grave in the urupā; a shabby old pavilion becomes the Blue Moon Dance Hall, boys lining up on one side and girls the other. Even a repetitive job on the folding machine has its interests and consolations. 'There were contrasting rhythms on the factory floor that lived somewhere in the bodies of those who worked there.'

Mavis stays when the whistle sounds and meticulously cleans and oils her machine. ('The Machine'). At home there is the bleak accusing voice of her mother; at work the closest to a friend is her supervisor, Syd. When her mother is admitted to hospital there is a castigating doctor: 'The words fell from his hostile mouth, pinching and spreading and bouncing like rubber bands.' Animate and inanimate connect as easily as the living addressing the dead.

If I have a favourite story it is 'Green Dress', in which all the virtues are crammed together. There's this at the beginning:

> These words, which are barred behind clamped-down teeth—teeth which have a pair of sealed-off lips to the fore of them— are not incarcerated here because of what I wore to my wedding. The colour green has nothing to do with what's happening right here, now, despite what my mother may think.

And then, out it comes, in dialogue: 'lame dogs, wet ducks, losers' are excoriated. 'He's got mad eyes.' Then it's the turn of mayhem, crying, a cop car in the cemetery. The last words are: 'Fingers crossed.'

★

On the night of the banquet in Alcalá we returned to Colegio Mayor de San Ildefonso, where several hands reached up to raise the heavy knocker and crash it down on the forbidding door. A voice from deep inside could be heard calling, 'I'm coming.' Soon we would be home again, taking the memory of acclaim, of ceremony, of as many academics as there were writers—and our sense of the short story as a form we could play with indefinitely.

In 'Whakarongo', cousins, one living, one non-living, exchange information on the state of the world and discuss seahorses. 'Anyway, dearest ones, you have the best spot—safe from rising tides, swelling rivers, fire, hurricanes, tornadoes, greed, motorways, rampaging viruses.' Final advice: 'Listen to the birds'.

Note
1. Ann Patchett, *These Precious Days* (Bloomsbury, 2021).

Genealogies Constitute Histories
David Eggleton

An Indigenous Ocean: Pacific essays by Damon Salesa (Bridget Williams Books, 2023), 388pp, $49.99

Why study history, and why study the history of the Indigenous Pacific in particular? To what uses might such studies be put? These are urgent and important questions implicitly addressed in Damon Salesa's new book, *An Indigenous Ocean: Pacific essays*, a collection of 'Pacific' essays originally published diversely between 2003 and 2014.

Here, history studies is shown to be a relevant institutional methodology. As Salesa argues in his Introduction, we—by which is meant those who live in the region and are concerned with the Indigenous—are 'in danger of losing the Pacific to the world'. Identity is both visceral and ideological, and at this moment in time fiercely contested through competing narratives, where 'history' breaks down into 'histories'. He adds: 'Indigenous scholars are doing more and more history and they are doing it less and less within the discipline of traditional history'—rather, it's as students of criminology, or law, or health.

Globally, the Pacific Ocean, the Moana, is the largest single physical feature on planet Earth, but as Salesa points out: 'Oceania is commonly invisible and seemingly illegible in most global narratives ... Omitted or divided or occluded, it is never seen whole.' Instead, it's part of the American lake, or part of the Pacific Rim, or part of the Indo-Pacific, or part of the Asia-Pacific. It is a geopolitical pawn on a chessboard in a United States-led attempt to counter the ubiquitous soft power of China.

Then there are the local tensions, such as France's largesse in bribing voters through inducements in French Polynesia to keep it as French territory. There are mass tourism invasions and environmental concerns raised by cheap air travel, cruise ships and global warming, while billionaire corporations buy up and control large archipelagoes, and populations are homogenised by globalisation into surveilled subjects.

There are a lot of paradoxes here and Oceania itself is a vexed term which Salesa does his best to unpack. Meanwhile, other historical categories for describing its geography are unsatisfactory: simplifying labels like 'Polynesia', 'Micronesia' and 'Melanesia' misrepresent the complexities of locations.

But in the face of eurocentric terminology and the 'Great Powers' grand narratives, and despite the economic creation beginning in the nineteenth century of 'an unequal ocean', Salesa, a compelling and knowledgeable Indigenous historian, shows us—through his heavily footnoted and referenced essays—the Indigenous societies of the region as resourceful, adaptable and durable. The Moana has always been a place of oppositions and contradictions and these societies had their own strategies for affirming and maintaining the mana of the people.

In the essay 'Alāva'a: Seaways across an Indigenous Ocean' he defines 'seaways' as 'known passages between places' across vast distances: 'the sea remains a point of fundamental orientation'. Expertly navigating their ocean-going canoes, different island groups established connections across the Moana through material trade and ceremonial exchange. Salesa adds that an earlier generation of Indigenous scholars—including Te Rangihīroa Sir Peter Buck, Epeli Hau'ofa and 'Okasitino Māhina—had stressed these connections, offering in this way 'interwoven archipelagic visions', while physical evidence remains in the form of altered anthropogenic landscapes. These include monoliths in Rapanui and Tonga and elsewhere; vast terracing seen from New Zealand to Tahiti; and irrigation networks from the New Guinea Highlands to Hawai'i. And now in the twenty-first century, networks of exchange and solidarity include the Pacific Games, the Pacific Arts Festival, the University of the South Pacific and the Pacific Islands Forum.

Then there are the traditional narratives that authenticate possession and continuity, beginning with the cosmological age of creation. 'This merges into an age of tribal ancestors which has elements of the fabulous ... This is succeeded by genealogical times past to which the present is connected through ancestors of the living.'

Expanding on the significance of

genealogies, Salesa explains that they themselves constitute histories. Genealogies are 'highly allusive, frequently esoteric or protected, and are political … in claims to lineage, property, office and chiefly titles'. But what has been damaging is colonial scholars remaking specific genealogies as sources for westernised histories that 'convert them to other terms'.

One of the themes or concerns throughout this collection is the changing ways in which Western scholarship has dealt with interactions between 'native and settler pasts', particularly in Australia and New Zealand, but Salesa also judiciously comments on American historical interpretations:

> While 'colonial' is a pejorative word in the Antipodes, in North America it is more often simply a marker of a foundational past, of a long-lost period, even of quaintness, and these divergent visions of the 'colonial' are juxtaposed when scholars of the Atlantic and the Antipodes encounter each other. A corrective to this has been historical narratives which put the history of slavery at the centre of the Atlantic world.

Another topic explored carefully and incrementally is 'New Zealand's Overseas Empire 1840–1945'—that is, the assorted and sometimes quirky manifestations of New Zealand's attempt to emulate Britain and create its own mini-empire in the South Pacific, with its various long-term results: 'New Zealand succeeded in orienting certain Pacific nations towards it permanently.'

The main rival to this empire-building was felt to be Australia. And though Governors William Hobson and George Grey, as well as New Zealand's first Anglican bishop, George Selwyn, all more or less 'had a sense of Pacific destiny for New Zealand', it was Premier Richard Seddon who sought to turn it into a coherent project. When in 1899 Sāmoa was divided between Germany and the United States, 'no-one took the loss of Sāmoa quite as hard as Richard Seddon … Consequently he sought the annexation of the Cook Islands, Tonga, Niue and Fiji.'

Damon Salesa offers examples of how Seddon's island-grabbing paternalism endures, including the observation that: 'Colonialism in the Pacific was punctuated and shaped by the personal whim of scattered New Zealand officials who were, not unfairly, characterised as Pooh-Bahs.'

Oceania is a hybrid entity, a cross-cultural intersection of genealogies, stories, religions, languages, in search, perhaps, of a common destiny. In Salesa's wide-ranging compendium of comparisons and contrasts there are no final conclusions, only open-ended discussion. He also notes that 'few places are more evidently global or transnational than Sāmoa or Tonga, with populations as large overseas as at home'—surely indicating that in an internet-connected age the world now, rather than a place of centres and peripheries, might be better understood as a web or mesh of interacting relationships: the centre is everywhere, although how far down it goes needs more exploration.

scorpio Books

YOUR INDEPENDENT
BOOK STORE

scorpiobooks.co.nz
03 379 2882

Lily, Oh Lily: Searching for a Nazi ghost
Jeffrey Paparoa Holman

$36.99, PB, 200pp

'Family memoir at full stretch, made with love, yearning and just a hint of reproach. A wise, timely, beautiful read.' —Diana Wichtel

'*Lily, Oh Lily* is a thriller, a search for a particular person caught in the events of Nazi Germany – not a whodunnit, but a where-is-she?' —Patrick Evans

 Canterbury University Press

Available from all good bookshops

www.canterbury.ac.nz/cup

The perfect match.
(That's what we do)

UNITY BOOKS AUCKLAND

Unity Books Auckland: 09 307 0731, shop@unitybooksauckland.co.nz
Unity Books Wellington: 04 499 4245, wellington@unitybooks.co.nz

unitybooks.co.nz

NEW BOOKS FROM OTATO UNIVERSITY PRESS

Find out more at oup.nz

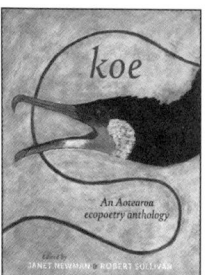

Koe: An Aotearoa ecopoetry anthology
Edited by Janet Newman and Robert Sullivan
PB | $50 | ISBN 9781990048814

This new anthology provides a comprehensive overview of the development and heritage of Aotearoa New Zealand's unique ecopoetry tradition. *Koe* features more than 100 poems of celebration, elegy, fear, hope and activism. Drawing from both traditional Māori poetry and the English poetry canon, these poems challenge traditional Eurocentric perspectives and wrestle with the impacts of European colonisation.

The Twisted Chain
by Jason Gurney
PB | $35 | ISBN 9781990048791

The Twisted Chain blends Jason Gurney's personal story about the impacts of rheumatic fever in his family with an exploration of the various causes of this disease. Gurney investigates the shockingly high rates of rheumatic fever in New Zealand's Māori and Pasifika communities, highlights the deep impact of the disease on individuals and whānau, and critiques the socio-political decisions that allow this preventable illness to persist in modern-day Aotearoa New Zealand.

Pretty Ugly
by Kirsty Gunn
PB | $35 | ISBN 9781990048890

Pretty Ugly by Kirsty Gunn is the inaugural title in a new series of short story collections from Landfall Tauraka and Otago University Press, celebrating the art of short fiction in Aotearoa New Zealand. These 13 stories, set in New Zealand and in the UK, are a testament to Gunn's unrivalled ability to look directly into the troubled human heart and draw out what dwells there.

Liar, Liar, Lick, Spit
by Emma Neale
PB | $30 | ISBN 9781990048883

Fibs, porkies, little white lies, absolute whoppers and criminal evasions: the ways we can deceive each other are legion. *Liar, Liar, Lick, Spit*, the new collection by Ōtepoti poet and writer Emma Neale, is fascinated by our doubleness. From the unwitting tricks our minds play, to the mischievous pinch of literary pastiche; from the corruptions of imperialism or abuse, to the dreams and stories we weave for our own survival, these poems catalogue scenes that seem to suggest our species could be named for its subterfuge as much as for its wisdom.

UNIVERSITY BOOK SHOP

For all booklovers, *everywhere.*

Dunedin's most loved independent book shop, full of beautiful books, elegant gifts, postal services and friendly booksellers.

378 Great King St
Dunedin North
03 477 6976
enquiries@unibooks.co.nz

Mon-Fri: 9am-5.30pm
Sat-Sun: 10am-4pm

www.unibooks.co.nz

LANDFALL
Young Writers' Essay Competition

Entries are now open for the 2025 Landfall Young Writers' Essay Competition.

The competition is open to anyone in Aotearoa aged 16–25 and will be judged by *Landfall* editor Lynley Edmeades.

The winner will receive $500 and a year's subscription to *Landfall*. They will also have their essay published in *Landfall 249*, coming out in May 2025.

Entries close 31 March 2025
Find out more at oup.nz/landfall-yw-essay-comp

Subscribe to *Landfall*: Supporting creativity in Aotearoa New Zealand since 1947

Be among the first to receive each new issue of Aotearoa New Zealand's most prestigious journal of arts and letters. For nearly 80 years, *Landfall* has been a vital platform for emerging and established writers and artists, showcasing the latest art, poetry, essays, fiction and reviews.

Subscribe today to receive *Landfall* 249 and our special 250th anniversary issue, *Landfall* 250.

For details on how to subscribe or become a Friend or Patron of this important toanga, see page 207.

LANDFALL

CONTRIBUTORS

Ambika G.K.R. is Tamilian, Indian, raised in Zambia and moved to Aotearoa as a teenager. She is an improviser, actor, sketch writer and comedian.

Philip Armstrong is the author of *Sinking Lessons* (Otago University Press, 2020), which won the Kathleen Grattan Award for Poetry in 2019. His poems and short stories have appeared in *Landfall*, *Sport*, *PN Review*, *Pleiades* and elsewhere. His second book of poetry, *Touch Screen*, will be published by Otago University Press in 2025.

Atareria is a writer based in Ōtautahi who keeps the North Island in her heart. Her whakapapa flows from Ngāti Pūkenga, Ngāti Maru, Te Rarawa, Éire and Latvija.

Hannah August works at a New Zealand university. She has published widely on Shakespeare and early modern English drama and reviewed books for RNZ, NZ Listener, *The Spinoff* and the *Times Literary Supplement*.

Tony Beyer is a writer based in Taranaki. His work has appeared in national and international journals and anthologies, and he is the author of a number of poetry collections.

Cindy Botha lives in Tauranga where she began writing at near 60. Her poems have appeared in magazines and anthologies in New Zealand, Australia, the UK and USA.

Heidi Brickell (Te Hika o Pāpāuma, Ngāti Kahungunu, Rangitāne, Rongomaiwahine, Ngāti Apakura) is an Ōtaki-based artist. Her art practice, grounded in the psychological and informed by her fascination with language as its vehicle, has been showcased in major contemporary art surveys at Auckland Art Gallery and Christchurch Art Gallery. Her work is held in major collections and she is represented by Laree Payne Gallery.

Diana Bridge's eighth collection, *Deep Colour*, came out from Otago University Press in 2023. A group of 'China-based' poems was included in *Encountering China*, an anthology of personal experiences of China also published in 2023.

Sholto Buck is a poet living in Melbourne. His first book, *In the Printed Version of Heaven*, was published by Rabbit in 2023. He has a PhD in creative writing from RMIT University.

Shelley Burne-Field is the 2024 Emerging Māori Writer in Residence at Te Herenga Waka Victoria University of Wellington. She is a children's novelist and short story writer. In 2023, she was the inaugural Pikihuia Poetry Award winner and Pasifika Sunday-Star Times Short Story Award winner.

Medb Charleton is originally from Ireland. She publishes poetry regularly in journals in Aotearoa New Zealand and is currently writing a novel.

Cadence Chung is a poet and composer studying at the New Zealand School of Music. She is the author of the nationally bestselling chapbook *anomalia* (Tender

Press, 2022) and an anthology of young artists, *Mythos* (Wai-te-ata Press, 2024).

Sherryl Clark is the author of *Mina and the Whole Wide World* (University of Queensland Press, 2021), which won the Australian Prime Minister's Literary Award for Children's Literature in 2022. Her latest crime novel is *Woman, Missing* (Harlequin Australia, 2024).

Kim Cope Tait is the author of the chapbook *Element* (Leaping Dog Press, 2005) and *Shadow Tongue* (Finishing Line Press, 2018). She is working on an English PhD with a critical/creative thesis at the University of Otago.

Elese Dowden is a Pākehā writer and scholar from Tāmaki Makaurau living on Wurundjeri land. Her poetry, essays and criticism have been published in *Cordite*, *Meanjin*, *Overland*, *Rabbit* and *Landfall*.

Breton Dukes lives in Ōtepoti with his wife and three boys. 'In the Company of Bullies' is an excerpt from a novel in progress, with the working title 'The Idea of Love'.

Mark Edgecombe is a church pastor in Tawa, Wellington, where he lives with Sarah and their three children.

David Eggleton is an Ōtepoti Dunedin-based writer of Rotuman, Tongan and Palangi heritage.

Rangi Faith (Kāi Tahu, Ngāti Kahungunu, English, Scottish) is a retired teacher living in Rangiora. His poetry explores European and Māori histories and has appeared in several recent anthologies and collections.

Holly Fletcher is a writer living in Ōtepoti Dunedin. She studied literature and creative writing at Goldsmiths, University of London. Holly's writing has been published in New Zealand and the UK.

Es Foong is a Malaysian-Chinese poet living on the lands of the Wurundjeri people. Their debut poetry collection *Clot and Marrow* was published in 2023.

Emma Gattey is a writer and critic from Ōtautahi. She is working on a PhD in New Zealand history at the University of Cambridge and is a Research Fellow for Te Takarangi.

Eliana Gray is a poet living in Ōtepoti. You can find their work in various places, including *The Spinoff*, *Overland*, *Poetry Aotearoa Yearbook* and *Cordite*.

Isabel Haarhaus is a writer and teacher in Tāmaki Makaurau. She has published short stories, poetry, essays, reviews, articles and art writing. Her collection of short stories, 'Feral', is under review with a publisher.

David Herkt is an Auckland-based writer, poet and journalist.

Michael Hulse is an English poet, translator, critic and anthologist who has enjoyed friendships with several New Zealand writers. He helped establish the Hippocrates Initiative, which awards the annual Hippocrates Prize for poetry on a medical subject.

Michael D. Jackson is a prize-winning poet and anthropologist. He is Senior Research Fellow in World Religions at Harvard Divinity School and the author of over 40 books, including *The Politics of Storytelling* (Chicago University Press, 2002) and *Beginnings* (Ugly Hill Press, 2024).

Erik Kennedy is the author of *Another Beautiful Day Indoors* (2022) and *There's No Place Like the Internet in Springtime* (2018), both with Te Herenga Waka University Press.

Brent Kininmont's second collection of poems, 'The Companion to Volcanology', will appear in 2025 with Te Herenga Waka University Press.

John Kinsella's recent books include the third volume of his collected poems, *Spirals (2014–2023)* (University of Western Australia Press, 2024), and the short story collection *Beam of Light* (Transit Lounge, 2024).

Megan Kitching is an Ōtepoti Dunedin poet. Her debut collection, *At the Point of Seeing* (Otago University Press, 2023), won the Jessie Mackay Prize in the 2024 Ockham New Zealand Book Awards, and was awarded the 2024 Laurel Prize Best International First Collection.

Jessica Le Bas has published two collections of poetry, *incognito* (2007) and *Walking to Africa* (2009), both with Auckland University Press. In 2019 she won the Sarah Broom Poetry Prize. Her prescient children's novel *Locked Down* was rereleased in 2021 by Penguin Random House. She lives in Rarotonga

Mary Macpherson is a Wellington poet, photographer, art writer and bookmaker. Her first poetry collection is *Social Media* (The Cuba Press, 2019).

Vana Manasiadis is a Greek-New Zealand writer based in Ōtautahi. She was the 2021 Ursula Bethell Writer-in-Residence at Te Whare Wananga o Waitaha University of Canterbury and now teaches creative writing there. Her latest book is *The Grief Almanac: A sequel* (Seraph Press, 2019).

Frankie McMillan is an award-winning poet and short story writer. Her latest book, *The Wandering Nature of Us Girls*, was published by Canterbury University Press in 2022. Her work appears in the *Best Microfiction* and *Best Small Fiction* anthology series.

Cilla McQueen MNZM, NZ Poet Laureate 2009–11, lives and writes in the southern port of Motupōhue, Bluff. Recent works are *In A Slant Light* (2016) and *Poeta* (2018), both from Otago University Press.

Josiah Morgan (Kāi Tahu, Ngāti Maniapoto) is a writer, performer and educator based in Ōtautahi. His latest poetry collection is *I'm Still Growing* (Dead Bird Books, 2024).

Janet Newman lives in Horowhenua. Her poetry collection *Unseasoned Campaigner* (Otago University Press, 2021) won the 2022 NZ Society of Authors' Heritage Book Award for Poetry. She is editor, with Robert Sullivan, of *Koe: An Aotearoa ecopoetry anthology* (Otago University Press, 2024).

Keith Nunes has had poetry, fiction, haiku and visuals published around the globe. He creates ethereal manifestations as a way of communicating with the outside world.

Rachel O'Neill is a filmmaker, writer and artist based in Te Whanganui-a-Tara. She authored *One Human in Height* (Hue & Cry Press, 2013) and *Requiem for a Fruit* (Tender Press, 2021), and was the 2023 Creative New Zealand Randell Cottage Writing Fellow.

Joanna Pascoe is a researcher at AUT, focusing on posthuman pedagogy, affirmative ethics, speculative fiction and poetic inquiry. She explores how speculative fiction may open lines of flight for an affirmative ethics of joy in education.

Jackson C. Payne is a writer and social worker from Aotearoa living on unceded Wurundjeri Woi Wurrung land in Naarm Melbourne. He holds a PhD in creative writing from Monash University.

Hannah Petuha is a writer and creative from Rangiuru, Te Puke. She is a MFA fiction candidate at Washington University in St Louis, where she now lives.

Perena Quinlivan (Ngāi Te Rangi, Ngāti Ranginui) is a Tāmaki Makaurau-based writer and poet working professionally in the areas of Māori economic and social development, whose writing often reflects these concerns.

Rebecca Reader is a Maid of Kent, having been born east of the River Medway in England. Her stories and poems took their first breaths in New Zealand, the UK and Latin America.

Brett Reid is a sports administrator living in Auckland. He has no collections unless you count two rusted steel rail spikes and five small smooth stones gathered on his travels.

Simon Richardson has worked as a full-time artist since graduating from Otago Polytechnic School of Art (BFA, 1996). He is a three-time winner of the Canadian Elizabeth Greenshields Foundation grant and was a finalist in the BP Portrait Award at the National Gallery London and the 2024 Archibald Awards.

Tess Ritchie is from Ōtepoti Dunedin and lives in Naarm Melbourne. She is studying for an MA in poetry at the International Institute of Modern Letters and has poetry in *Sweet Mammalian* and forthcoming in *Australian Poetry Journal* and *Rabbit Poetry*.

Christopher Schmelz is an artist and musician from Koputai Port Chalmers, predominantly working with analogue film in both moving image and still photography, focusing on alternative hand development with caffenol.

Elizabeth Smither is a poet, novelist and short story writer. She is a former New Zealand Poet Laureate and has received numerous other awards. In 2018, her collection *Night Horse* won the poetry category of the Ockham New Zealand Book Awards.

Robert Sullivan (Kāi Tahu, Ngāpuhi, Irish) is an award-winning poet and children's writer. His most recent collections are *Tunui Comet* (2022) and *Hopurangi / Songcatcher: Poems from the*

Maramataka (2024), both with Auckland University Press. He co-edited with Janet Newman *Koe: An Aotearoa ecopoetry anthology* (Otago University Press, 2024). He is an associate professor of creative writing at Massey University and a great fan of all kinds of decolonisation.

Stayci Taylor is a senior lecturer at RMIT University. She teaches creative writing and media production alongside her research in screenwriting, nonfiction and queer screen. With a theatre and TV background, Stayci is drawn to playful collaborations in her writing and research life.

Philip Temple is an award-winning author of fiction and non-fiction books. He received a Prime Minister's Award for Literary Achievement in 2005 and has been appointed an Officer of the New Zealand Order of Merit for his services to literature.

Franchesca Walker (Ngāti Rakaipaaka, Ngāti Pāhauwera, Pākehā) grew up in Aotearoa but is gradually learning to call Australia home. She has been published on both sides of the Tasman, most recently in *Westerly*, *SBS Voices* and *Headland*.

Anna Woods' fiction has appeared in journals and anthologies; been shortlisted for the Commonwealth Short Story Prize; and won the Sargeson Prize. She holds a Master of Creative Writing from the University of Auckland, for which she wrote a novel.

Kirby Wright was born and raised on the remote Hawaiian island of Moloka'i.

CONTRIBUTIONS

Landfall publishes original poems, essays, short stories, excerpts from works of fiction and non-fiction in progress, reviews, articles on the arts, and portfolios by artists. Submissions must be emailed to landfall@otago.ac.nz with 'Landfall submission' in the subject line.

For further information visit our website oup.nz/landfall

SUBSCRIPTIONS

Landfall is published in May and November, Subscribing to *Landfall* helps to support Aotearoa New Zealand's longest running journal of arts and literature, and the writers and artists it showcases. Annual subscription rates for 2025 (two issues) are: New Zealand $65 (including GST); Australia $NZ75; rest of the world $NZ95. Institution, Friend or Patron subscriptions are also available.

For subscription enquiries and renewals, email press.accounts@otago.ac.nz or call +64 3 479 8807.

Print ISBN: 978-1-99-004886-9
ePDF ISBN: 978-1-99-004887-6
ISSN 00-23-7930

Copyright © Otago University Press 2024

Published by Otago University Press, Te Whare Tā o Ōtākou Whakaihu Waka 533 Castle Street, Dunedin New Zealand

Typeset by Otago University Press. Printed in New Zealand by Caxton.

Christopher Schmelz, *Chicks Hotel*, 2023, caffenol developed silver gelatin print, 24cm x 16cm.